Dedication

To Marlene, Suzanne, Monique, and Alfred:

Thank you so much for the awesome critiques. Your help has been invaluable in moving this series along.

To Mum & Dad:

Thank you for being such great fans through this crazy path I'm travelling.

To Andrew:

You're the best husband, friend, travelling companion, and book formatter a girl could hope for. Thank you for being excited about my Orphan Train books. I love you to the moon and back.

❧ BOOK 2 ❧

Orphan Train Series

Wendy May Andrews

ೞ

Sparrow Ink
www.sparrowink.com

Stay in touch with Wendy May Andrews
and forthcoming publishing news.

Sign up for her biweekly newsletter

Chapter One

As she stepped down from the train, Cassie quickly looked around and couldn't prevent the momentary scowl of distaste that covered her face before she smoothed out her features. It seemed the bright sun had bleached all color from the landscape, which was surprising since the train had passed enough bodies of water that everything should be perfectly lush. Every building in the small town was a dull gray. She supposed they just didn't much care about making it attractive. They had practicalities to worry about as they tried to expand and grow their enterprises. Cassie wrinkled her nose again as thoughts flitted through her mind, wondering what sort of activities kept the folks of Bucklin, Missouri busy. Clearly it wasn't painting their storefronts or planting flowers.

As she looked around, she saw the new arrivals were drawing considerable attention. It appeared even the townspeople were bleached out. There was very little color other than gray or brown wherever her gaze landed. Except for the piercing blue eyes of a disturbingly handsome man that seemed to be watching her intently.

Cassie shook her head and wrenched her eyes from the attractive face. "What have I done?" she asked herself for at least the tenth time in the past ten days. Her straw hat, which provided perfectly adequate protection in New York, was insufficient to keep her from squinting as she gazed about under the bright afternoon sun. She lifted her hand to provide a bit more shade for her eyes and a scowl marred her features once again as she saw how grubby her gloves had become.

That will teach you never to leave without a spare pair, won't it? she thought to herself with a slightly sardonic twist of her lips.

She forced her attention away from such senseless worries and back to the youngster holding tightly to her other hand. Cassie forced a cheerful smile to her lips and took a deep breath.

"Doesn't the air smell lovely here? Nothing like in New York, is it, Wally?"

Wally's worried face rearranged itself into a grin as he shook his head vigorously. "Do you think we'll like it here, Miss Cassie?"

Cassandra Marie Victoria Morley blinked at her young charge for a moment, and she swallowed the lump that had appeared suddenly in her throat. "I am quite convinced that you shall love it here, my dear boy. Now come along, all of you. We must gather our things and join the others. Let's not dawdle. The other children will be getting restless, and we don't want to keep the manager waiting. Your brand new lives await."

She was once again swept with awe and gratitude for the resilience of children. The six boys who had been entrusted to her accepted her feigned enthusiasm and quickly gathered their meager belongings. Cassie forced her eyes not to linger on the sight of her six charges and their small bundles of clothing. The anticipation and trepidation warring in their eyes caused the lump in her throat to grow and she couldn't allow them to see her distress. She covered her momentary weakness with brusque movement.

Tightening her grasp on Wally with one hand and her own bundle with the other, she admonished the other boys to stay close to her as they hurried to join the others. Unconsciously she found herself once again counting heads to make sure everyone was there. This wasn't her responsibility, of course, but she knew she would be unable to cope with the distress if they were to misplace any of the youngsters.

Finally, genuine amusement was able to make its way through the quagmire of her feelings while she watched the antics of some of the boys as they took advantage of being out in the open air after ten days cooped up on the train. It was futile for her to remind them to keep their clothes clean, but some of the other women were trying their best. Once again Cassie congratulated herself on the exercises she had made her boys do multiple times each day. She was quite certain it was the only reason the six were managing to contain themselves and remain by her side. That and the fact that her six were amongst the youngest of the large group, and they were still fearful of getting lost or separated from the familiar.

Her heart wrenched again. Cassie cleared her throat and blinked vigorously.

"Are you all right, Miss Cassie?" Wally's little hand tugged on her.

"I am perfectly fine, my dear. I think some dust got in my eye is all." Her explanation satisfied the small boy before their attention was snagged by the approach of a large, red-faced man.

"Welcome, welcome," he boomed, obviously wanting to appear jolly. "I apologize that I was not here before the train's arrival. It seems it arrived a little ahead of schedule."

Cassie grinned as she saw Melanie check her watch and sniff skeptically. Her amusement died quickly when she remembered that her boys' fates rested in this man's seemingly incompetent hands. She tried to shake her negative thoughts and determined to wait and see what would unfold.

"You must be the manager." Mrs. Parker stated the obvious, but Cassie knew it gave her a sense of control, so she tried not to allow her amusement to show. "We are more than ready to follow your lead, sir. What arrangements have been made for the children?"

"Well it is good that you arrived when you did. It will give us time to feed them all a little bit so they aren't too rambunctious before their new families arrive. The last train load I oversaw in another town didn't go very well because they were late and the youngsters were hungry and tired and cranky. We don't want to repeat that experience." The man's discomfort was apparent, and Cassie almost felt sympathetic for him at that moment, if not for the fact that he had yet to look at any of the boys. She wondered if he even liked children.

Mrs. Parker must have had serious doubts about the manager's competence, but there was nothing they could do at this point. She met the eyes of all the women with her as she looked around comprehensively. With a nod she took charge.

"You are Mr. McDonald, correct?" He had not introduced himself, and she was not about to follow a stranger out of the train station.

"Yes, yes, where are my manners? I do apologize. I was just so flummoxed from being late. You are Mrs. Parker, if I'm not mistaken?"

"That is correct. Very well, Mr. McDonald, lead us to whatever you have prepared for us. You are right in your assessment that the children would appreciate a meal and a chance to recover from the movement of the train before we proceed any further."

Without much more delay, they collected even the most rambunctious of the boys and made their way from the station.

By now Cassie's eyes had adjusted, for the most part, to the bright light, and she allowed herself to gaze about at the sights that confronted her. It was amazing to see how primitive it was. It felt like she had stepped back in time. One would think that by 1854 nowhere would be quite this backward. Obviously she was even more spoiled by her high life in New York than she had realized. It struck her as odd that there wasn't a single brick in sight. The strangeness of it all made her nervous, but she tried to hide her reaction from the others, ensuring that no one noticed her trepidation.

She could feel the interest their arrival had stirred in the tiny little town and was uncomfortably aware of many eyes examining her. Cassie lifted her chin, tightened her hold on the small hand in hers, and followed the others as they made their way from the station.

$$\wp\wr$$

He watched the large group as they made their way from the station. Everyone in the area would easily be able to tell who they were. Most, in fact, were anticipating adding to their households with at least one of the new arrivals. He hadn't realized the children would be accompanied by ladies, not that he had given the matter much thought. Now that he was thinking on it, it made sense that the children would not be able to travel on their own. He wondered what manner of woman would accompany a bunch of orphans to their new home. The ones he had noticed seemed to be widely varying. The young-looking one had certainly caught his eye. She had actually looked slightly familiar. It was probably just her New York attitude that had been clearly stamped on her face and had almost marred her beauty.

Charles gave his head a shake. He was not in the market for a wife. Women were nothing but trouble. That was why he was interested in some of the boys who had just arrived. A man in his position needed to have sons. This was the best way to get one, or more, without cluttering up his life with a woman.

Straightening from the post he had been leaning upon, Charles shoved his hat back on his head after wiping away the perspiration that had gathered. If it was already this hot in April, it didn't bode well for what kind of summer they'd be having. There was no sense in standing around; they wouldn't be gathering the children until later that afternoon.

But despite his determination, he could not prevent his eyes from following the young woman's progress as she made her way down the sidewalk. He should have been turned off by the look of revulsion he had seen on her face as she gazed about at the town. He had no interest in high maintenance city girls. Her fancy clothes and disapproving glance told him she was far too complicated for the likes of him. But it had also been impossible to miss the tender look she had bestowed upon the boys in her care. And her physical beauty was downright arresting. Besides, he reasoned with himself, she would obviously not be staying in town for more than a couple of days; there was no harm in feasting his eyes upon her. Convinced, he relaxed back into a slouch in the shade of the overhang in front of the saloon.

His curiosity was stirred by the new arrivals. He hadn't expected so many children to be accompanied by so few adults, and only women at that. He wondered again what manner of woman would have volunteered for such a task. The one he had noticed most appeared to be quite young despite the scowl that had painted her face. Her curly, yellow hair had reflected the sun's rays in quite a fascinating manner. He couldn't quite see the color of her eyes, as they were shaded by her bonnet, but he couldn't help but note her slender build. *Such a wispy little thing wouldn't last longer than a couple days in an environment such as this*, he thought with another shake of his head.

It didn't matter much to him, he insisted to himself. No woman was going to be his responsibility, especially not out here in the wilds of Missouri. He reminded himself once more that he loved the wilds of Missouri and ignored the motivations that kept his eyes fixed to the retreating form of the beautiful young woman from the train.

ᎦᏬ

"Why are so many people watching us, Miss Cassie?"

Cassie glanced down at the boy by her side and strove for a neutral expression. "There aren't very many people around, Wally, so there aren't that many watching us."

"But all of them are watching us."

She couldn't argue with the youngster's words. Everyone *was* watching them. It looked to her as though the entire population of the small town had turned out to observe their arrival.

"They probably don't get very many visitors around here, so they're curious about us. Besides, all these handsome young men to look at, they cannot help but stare." She realized her explanation was probably the truth. The further west they had travelled, the more sparsely populated the countryside had become. And they had arrived at the most western stop of the train line. She had heard the train company was planning to lay more track, but for now, this was as far as you could go by train. If you wanted to go any further west, you would have to travel by wagon. The thought of any more travel turned her stomach sour. The thought of being this isolated also made her shiver. But she didn't want Walter or his brothers to sense her discomfort, so she quickly continued talking.

"This is also the first time Mr. Brace has sent any of the orphans this far away, so it's very new for this town. It is to be expected that everyone would be curious."

"Are they going to like us, Miss Cassie?"

"They are going to love you, my dear boy. They will not be able to help themselves." She let go of his hand and pulled him closer to her side in a quick hug. Conscious of his manly pride despite being only six, she didn't prolong the contact and quickly let him go. She could see he appreciated the gesture by his bashful smile and the glance she received from him from beneath his eyelashes.

Both shaking themselves from the sentimental moment, they hurried to catch up with the others.

Chapter Two

Cassie watched Mr. McDonald closely as he wandered around the room. She could tell the man was trying to appear as though he were taking an interest in everyone, but she hadn't detected even an ounce of warmth in him as he spoke briefly to the boys who were huddling near her. Her heart constricted as she thought of the fear the youngsters were valiantly trying to hide. The round, balding man had gone to no effort to alleviate the fear that anyone with eyes could have seen written on their faces.

"Will you be heading back to New York on the next train?" Katie asked, making Cassie jump since she had not noticed her approach, so caught up was she in worrying about the incompetence of the manager.

Cassie turned to the other woman with a smile. "I don't think so."

"Your parents are going to be furious," Katie warned.

"They are going to be furious no matter what. Staying here a little longer isn't going to make any difference. In fact, it might help if it allows them time to get over their initial upset." Cassie couldn't help her negligent shrug. She really wasn't overly concerned about her parents' feelings on the matter. She had notified them of her intentions. If they didn't like it, that was their problem, not hers.

"I would have thought you would be anxious to get back to your life in the city," Katie persisted, obviously perplexed by the younger woman's decision to remain in the small town. "Is this not a rather backward place for you?"

Cassie huffed an impatient breath. "Of course it is. It's a backward place for all of us," she reminded her companion. "Are you overwhelmed with a desire to remain here for the scenery?"

It was obvious from her expression that Katie agreed, but she still argued, "I would imagine the scenery would be quite beautiful if it wasn't so dry and hot. But I always planned on staying. You never even intended to come. So I'm curious as to what could persuade you to be so long gone from your comfortable life back home."

Cassie held her breath and counted to ten, trying to swallow down the surge of anger she felt over the other woman's words. She couldn't really blame Katie for her opinion. Miss Cassandra Morley was a New York debutante, the spoiled only daughter of a wealthy landowner. This was quite decidedly not her usual milieu. And the other woman probably couldn't imagine why anyone would leave her life, even for a brief time. But volunteering at the orphanage, something she had originally done to prevent people from thinking her a complete egoist, had become the highlight of her days. She had become so attached to the children, and when she had found out some of her charges were being sent on the next orphan train, she had felt compelled to accompany them in order to ensure they found good homes.

She had begged her parents to adopt a few of the children. They had refused. Of course, Cassie was well aware the problem was too large for her parents to be able to solve it on their own, but she had been appalled by their attitude toward the poor abandoned waifs. She knew this fresh start in the Midwest was the children's best chance for a good life. Provided the incompetent manager undertook to get them placed, that is. There was no way Cassie could leave until she was sure her darlings were going to be well cared for. She would deal with the consequences of her parents' anger later.

Returning her attention to Katie's question, Cassie hoped her polite smile had not slipped. "Just as you are curious, so am I, Katie. I find I cannot bear to head back until I know for certain that the children will prosper."

There was enough truth in her answer to give it the twang of sincerity, and Cassie blew a small sigh of relief when Katie merely threw her a slightly puzzled glance before her attention was turned by a question one of the youngsters had posed. Cassie allowed her gaze to return to Mr. McDonald. She tried to keep a frown from forming on her face as she watched him talking with some of the townspeople. With another sigh, she realized she would have to write a letter to Mr. Brace warning him of the manager's unsavory demeanor. Cassie was worried his manner would turn off sincere folks who wanted to help the children while attracting those who might exploit the defenceless orphans.

"You aren't developing a tender for Mr. McDonald, are you, my dear girl? Surely with all the gentlemen present this evening, you could find a more worthy object for your affections."

Cassie gasped over the audacious words and the impudence of the one uttering them. She tried to ignore the shiver that threatened to slither up her spine over the delicious, deep timbre of the low, male voice near her ear. She turned to confront the speaker, shocked and dismayed to find it was the handsome man she had seen across the street from the train station when they arrived.

She was repulsed by his implication, despite the veracity of his words. In her opinion, nearly any man would be more worthy than Mr. McDonald. But the stranger's impudence could not be tolerated. The man deserved a set down.

Pulling herself to her tallest height, which she couldn't help noticing was still only around his chin level, Cassie gazed down her nose in her best imitation of her mother's proud stance. "My affections are none of your concern."

To her chagrin, it did not have the desired effect. The bounder laughed, which made her feel as though her blood was about to boil. She could feel hot color flooding her cheeks, but she decided to ignore it and him. She turned on her heel and marched over to Miss Melanie Jones.

Trying to hide her discomfort over the stranger's words, Cassie asked Miss Jones for a progress report. "Do you know what the delay is, Miss Mel? I understood this meeting was set to commence at 3:30. It is now 3:40."

Cassie was instantly soothed by the other woman's calm smile. "As I understand it, things are not always as organized as we are accustomed to out here in the wilds, my dear Cassie. It would seem Mr. McDonald is expecting more people to turn up, and he doesn't want to start without them."

Cassie glanced around once more, noting the people milling around, speaking to the children. "I guess it would be best if there are more people. I'm not sure if there are enough here right now to look after our lot."

"Unless some of them are planning to take more than one."

"Do you think anyone would be willing to take more than one boy? It would be wonderful if Wally and his brothers could be placed together." Cassie hadn't wanted to give voice to her deepest concern before then.

"I pray you don't get your hopes up, my dear. Three young boys would be a lot to take on for most people."

"I know, Melly, but the thought of those boys being separated from one another nearly breaks my heart."

The other woman apparently didn't have any wisdom to offer because she merely grasped Cassie's hand in a warm clasp for a moment before they drifted away from one another to check once more on the children. The boys were getting restless and needed to be distracted in order to keep them on their best behavior while still on display in front of their potential new families.

As much as Cassie thought this was a great opportunity for the children to find new homes and a better future than the stews of New York had offered them, the experience of watching strangers examining her charges put her in mind of a retail experience, and she was beginning to find it repugnant. She was quite certain she would not be returning to repeat the experience ever again. Perhaps she would have to find a new project when she returned home, as this one was threatening to be a heart breaking one.

"Are my new parents here, Miss Cassie?" Walter asked her anxiously.

"I surely hope so, Wally," she answered with as much positivity as she could infuse into her voice.

"Which ones are they?" he asked, his eager eyes darting around the room.

"Heavens, I don't know. We'll have to wait and see what Mr. McDonald says. Oh, hush now, it looks as though he's finally going to get things under way."

Cassie watched and tried to keep the skepticism from her face as the placement agent stepped to the front of the room and cleared his throat loudly.

"Good afternoon, everyone. Thank you so much for coming. We have a roomful of youngsters here that could use your help and are looking forward to being a part of your lives."

Cassie stifled her sigh. The words he was saying were great — if only he could inject a note of sincerity into his voice, she might actually believe that he meant it. She bit her lip to prevent any tears from forming as she glanced at the boys by her side. As she was returning her gaze to the speaker, it was snagged by the handsome cowboy who had been so rude to her. He was watching her intently, so she shot a scowl at him before dragging her attention back to what Mr. McDonald was saying.

ℰℭ

The young woman was so beautiful it made him uncomfortable. Charles fought his grin. She was obviously one of those females who was always changing her mind about how she felt. There weren't nearly enough women this far from the East Coast — why did such a complicated one have to turn up in his town? He had the impression she was a spoiled little rich girl, but then he saw her tenderness with the youngsters in her charge and was amazed at how the boys huddled around her. They were too young to be responding to her beauty. *They must actually like the young woman*, he marvelled, as he struggled to maintain his neutral expression after she sent that glare in his direction. She was obviously determined to keep him in his place.

It had not been well of him to be vulgar towards her earlier, but she brought out such strange reactions in him. He did not doubt it was the air of monied privilege that hung about her, despite her association with the orphans. He hadn't even had a conversation with her, but he had heard her speak. Her accent and vocabulary, besides the obvious quality of her now travel-worn clothes, all screamed privileged background. He wondered how the poor dear was managing so far from the gilded halls she had obviously grown up in. He searched his memory, trying to determine why she looked so familiar. She was far too young to have been an acquaintance of his. Perhaps he knew her parents.

Charles dragged his attention away from its infatuation with the beautiful blonde and endeavored to focus on what the manager was saying. Despite how irritating he found the other man, Charles was determined to collect a few of the children for himself. It was a worthy cause and the only way he could envision himself achieving the status of father figure. And to be sure, his spread could use some extra hands to help, even if they were little ones.

Thankfully the dull-witted agent kept his message short, merely reminding everyone of what they had agreed to in relation to the boys – namely to educate them and provide for them as though they were members of the family until they reached the age of seventeen years. Charles glanced around and observed varying degrees of agreement amongst the assembled crowd. He'd had no trouble getting members of the committee to vouch for him, but he wondered how some of those present had managed to get anyone to agree to entrust them with young lives. He made a mental note to keep an eye out for some of the others. He wished he could take the entire lot of youngsters, but he reminded himself once more that was not a liveable solution.

Now the agent was reading out the names of the new parents that had already been matched up with some of the boys. Charles looked around, anxious to know who would be joining his life. He was surprised when there was a stir around the beautiful blonde after his name was read followed by the names of three boys.

"Did you hear that, Miss Cassie? We get to stay together."

She quickly hushed him, but Charles could see that she was not unaffected by the news. Her smile had begun to wobble, and he could see the tears welling in her eyes that she quickly blinked away. Charles did not want to find her any more appealing than he already did. Seeing her as a warm, compassionate woman did not help him. He gritted his teeth and determined to ignore her.

That was far easier said than done. When Mr. McDonald stopped talking, Charles had to go meet the boys who would be coming home with him. Unfortunately, they were still clinging to the beautiful blonde. He forced himself to approach her once more as he fought the urge to apologize for his previous behavior.

"Hello," he began, after clearing his throat to alleviate his unexpected nervousness.

He could see that she was trying to ignore him, but the boys by her side did not do so.

"Are you going to be our father?"

Charles looked down into the earnest young faces and felt his hardened heart crack just a little bit. "I sure hope so — if you'll have me," he answered. "What's your name?"

"I'm Anton, but you can call me Tony," came the reply. "These two are Walter and Ross. They're twins. They're six. I just turned ten."

"It's a pleasure to meet the three of you, Tony. Are you ready to go?"

This question brought a quiet sound of distress from the one member of the group he had not yet acknowledged, forcing his eyes to search her face. He could see that she was trying to hide her reaction, but she obviously had not expected them to be leaving her side so soon. It was also apparent that she was embarrassed to have revealed her feelings. Charles was amused to see her efforts to place a glare back onto her face despite her wet eyes.

"Where is your wife?" she asked, her tone accusing.

"I don't have one."

His reply made her blink. "How do you intend to care for these boys on your own?"

"Well, they strike me as fine young men that shan't require a mother, since they're clearly big enough to be house broken."

He had to bite his tongue to control his laughter as hot color rose in her neck and cheeks. He could tell she wanted to smack him but was too polite to do so. It was fascinating to watch her try to draw her composure around herself.

"Are you quite sure you are prepared to take three youngsters into your home all at once? Perhaps there was some sort of mistake with Mr. McDonald." Her feelings were clearly torn on the subject. Charles guessed that she wouldn't want the boys to be taken away from each other, but she doubted his ability to care for them.

"No mistake, ma'am," he replied politely, keeping a straight face before he took pity on her and explained. "I had originally signed up for two boys, but when I heard about these three brothers, I figured there wouldn't be very many who'd be in a position to add three to their household, and it would be terrible for them to be broken up. So I said I'd be happy to have them."

Her face now grew even more suspicious. "What does a single man want with three boys?"

Charles was becoming tired of her issues. "Not that it's any of your business, ma'am, but I have a large spread that I could use some sons to help me with. Seeing as I don't have a wife, this is the best way for me to gain some."

Seeing her expression soften once more only served to irritate Charles, so he turned his shoulder to her and crouched down in front of the younger two boys. "Do you have all of your stuff with you, or do we need to go somewhere to pick it up? I would just as rather get going so we can get you nicely settled before it gets dark."

"We have our stuff with us, mister. We didn't have very much to bring," Ross answered while Walter turned his face into the blonde's skirt.

She quickly kneeled down in front of the boy. "Oh, Wally, don't you worry. This nice man is going to take you and your brothers home with him. I bet he has some lovely horses he'll let you help him with. Isn't that right, mister?" She broke off as their eyes met. Charles let the silence drag for a moment as he almost got lost in her bottomless gaze.

That silence was broken as the youngster still clinging to her asked, his voice plaintive, "But aren't you going to come with us, Miss Cassie?"

Chapter Three

C assie felt as though her heart was being wrung right out of her chest with Walter's question. The silence stretched for an uncomfortable moment before she kneeled down in front of the boy.

"My dear, you do realize that you're going to stay with Mister—" there was a pause while she digested the fact that she didn't even know the man's name. She quickly carried on. "You're going to go stay with this nice man. I bet he's actually a real, live cowboy. You are going to love it at his house." She bit her lip, willing her tears to stay away, praying that she was not lying to the little boy.

"But I want you to come, too," the little boy insisted, his tone starting to become a bit querulous.

The only thing Cassie could do was pull him into her arms and give him a tight hug. "I know, my darling, but I can't come to stay with you."

When he pulled back from her arms and looked at her with tears welling in his eyes, Cassie's heart cracked, and she looked at the cowboy in desperation. She didn't know what to do about the fact that he merely gazed back at her, showing no reaction to her plight or the child's distress. Now Cassie had another thing to worry about. *Will these dear boys be in good hands with this man? I never should have volunteered at the orphanage*, she thought in despair, but it was far too late for that, she already cared too deeply for the children. She would have to stay in town long enough to ensure they were well cared for. While she had grown closest to Walter and his brothers, Cassie was concerned for all the children they had brought with them.

With that determination, Cassie stood and turned to the taciturn man watching her. A part of her wanted to turn on her heel and sweep from the building without ever giving the man a second thought, but if he was going to have the care of the boys, she would have to swallow her pride and make peace with him.

She tried for a conciliatory smile and put her hand out to shake his. After a brief hesitation, he engulfed her small hand in his warm one. The sensation was distracting, but Cassie ignored it. "My name is Cassandra Morley. I fear I was so caught up with the children that I failed to introduce myself."

Cassie was surprised to see that the man looked as though he wished to ignore her introduction, but he must've been raised properly and his inborn manners won out. "I'm Charles Ainsworth." He kept his response as brief as possible.

Swallowing back her ire, Cassie was sure her smile was slipping and did her best not to grimace at the uncommunicative cowboy. "Would it be acceptable with you, Mr. Ainsworth, if I were to visit the boys a time or two before I leave town? It might help them adjust to their new surroundings" —she paused for a moment before admitting in a rush— "and I've grown rather fond of them and find I cannot yet bear to say goodbye."

She was surprised to see him appear to soften toward her but then thought it had been all in her imagination as he began to frown. She thought he was going to refuse her request and was preparing to argue when he again surprised her by agreeing. "There shouldn't be any harm in you stopping by. Anyone in town will be able to give you directions."

She dipped her head in acknowledgement, not bothering to say anything as the man was obviously not overly fond of words. Instead she kneeled down next to Walter once more.

"See now, Wally my dear, it is settled. You go with your brothers with Mr. Ainsworth, and I will come and see you. You will have so much to tell me and show me when I come to visit you. Won't that be lovely?"

Walter didn't look completely convinced, but he finally let go of her and followed his brothers as they were being ushered out by their new guardian. Cassie had to turn away so she wouldn't give way to tears. She didn't know how she would be able to enforce it, but that man had better treat her boys well or she would figure out a way to make him pay, she thought with a fierce protectiveness she had never felt before.

Struggling to maintain her composure, Cassie turned away, not able to watch as the boys left with their new guardian. She was grateful to see Mrs. Parker approach. Hopefully she had an assignment for her. She could use the distraction.

℘)(℘

Charles breathed a sigh of relief as soon as they were away from the lovely blonde. It had been obvious to him that she was distressed about saying goodbye to the children, but she had been valiantly trying to hide her feelings. He did not want to find her attractive and had to fight the urge to comfort her. Maybe he should have allowed the boys longer to say their goodbyes to her, but he doubted drawing it out would have made it any less painful. And he had been correct about why she had looked familiar to him. He was fairly certain he had met her father. It wasn't likely there were too many rich Morleys in New York City.

"So do you have horses, Mr. Charles?" the little guy asked him. What was his name? Oh yes, Walter.

"I have lots of them, Walter," he answered, startled when he felt a small hand slipping into his. He didn't think he had ever held a child's hand before. It made the strangest sensation spread in his chest. Instinctively, he wanted to let go but knew that would hurt the boy's feelings and damage their chances of developing a relationship. Charles rather thought the boy was a little old for wanting to hold hands. Even his twin brother was hurrying along, trying to swagger like the older boy. On further consideration, though, Charles thought that the loss of his parents might have made him more emotionally fragile. He was going to have to think about how to help the youngsters deal with their loss and settle into life here on the prairies. Maybe he should have talked with the young woman a little longer. She was probably more in touch with feelings than he was.

But she was also a beautiful, young woman from the city, and she would have no idea how to ease these boys into life on his spread. He was on his own with this challenge. He reminded himself that he was an intelligent, competent, successful man. He could manage these three youngsters just fine on his own. And he wouldn't be truly on his own, anyway. There were all his hired hands that helped on his spread. Surely they would be of assistance. The boys would love them as much as he did, he was sure.

He realized the boy was still gazing at him expectantly, and he thought back to their conversation. They had been talking about horses.

"Have you ever ridden on a horse?"

The vigorous shaking of the boy's head lead Charles to wonder if he would be afraid of horses.

"Have you ever seen a horse up close?"

"No," was the response, accompanied by more head shaking.

"Do you want to?"

Finally there was some nodding of his head. Charles felt relief spread through him. "Well now you'll get your chance. We'll have to ride in my wagon to get home, and it's pulled by two horses."

"Will they like me?"

Charles stifled a sigh. His misgivings were correct. The youngster had all sorts of negative feelings that would have to be sorted out, poor little mite. "I'm sure they will. They're fairly reasonable nags. If you were to offer them a carrot or an apple, they'd probably be your friend for life."

"But I don't have any carrots or apples," Walter worried.

"I've got plenty at home, don't worry. Now come along, your brothers are going to get away on us." Charles was relieved to note that this worked magically on the boy to hurry him along. Within moments, they joined Ross and Tony and reached the Smithy where he had left his wagon.

All three boys were pretty excited about the horses, making Charles glad he had brought that particular pair. He had other, more excitable horses that would have found the attention a bit much. But the two mature mares took it all in stride, almost as though they recognized how young the boys were and thus their inexperience was tolerable.

Before long they were all loaded up and rattling their way along the rutted road toward his property. The boundary of his property wasn't too terribly far from the town, but it would take them a little while to get to the house. The laughter from the boys as they bounced around in the back of the wagon reminded him that he ought to do something about how rough the road was. He mentally added one more item to the long list of things he needed to do.

He was content with his decision to add the youngsters to his household, no matter how much work they might be. He was tired of being alone out here on the prairies. He did not regret his decision to leave his old life behind and usually enjoyed the solitude this vast land offered, but he was glad that he would now have others to share his life with. And a man ought to have heirs to leave the fruitage of his hard work to, whether they were of his own blood or not. His parents would never agree with such a sentiment, but he couldn't be bothered to care about their thoughts on the matter. He shook himself from the maudlin train of thought and tried to engage the boys in conversation.

"Tell me about yourselves, boys," he began. The silence that followed reminded him that this was too broad of a conversation starter, especially when dealing with youngsters. He glanced back to see how they were reacting.

Charles had to stifle the urge to chuckle over their wide-eyed confusion as they nudged one another, urging the oldest to say something. He spoke up, focusing the conversation.

"Have the three of you been in school?"

Now Tony spoke for all of them. "Yes," he answered briefly at first, but when Charles remained silent, the boy elaborated. "When I was little, our mother taught me, but then when we were on the street, after our parents died, none of us could go to school. We learned lots on the street, but it's not what most would consider proper. Then Mr. Brace, the man who arranged for us to come on the train, is really big on schooling. He doesn't have much care for anyone who doesn't want to learn. He says learning's the only way we're going to get ourselves anywhere in life."

"He sounds like a wise man," Charles commented. He thought he ought to comment on the loss of their parents but wasn't sure what to say. While he was still debating with himself, the boy continued.

"But look how far we've come, and I don't see how it has anything to do with learning."

Charles again had to stifle his amusement over the boy's reasoning.

"Mr. Brace sounds like he must be a well-educated man. You came all this way because of his success. But you're still youngsters. If you want to have your own success when you're grown up, you'll need an education for that."

"Miss Cassie says the same thing. She was pretty nice about it, but she still insisted we had to do our studies, even on the train. Even during the first couple days when Ross' tummy felt poorly, Miss Cassie made us read to him. She said it was probably just the movement of the train making him sick and it was just his tummy, not his brain, so he could still learn."

Now Charles couldn't hold back his laughter. The boy sounded so aggrieved by this strange adult behavior. But Charles wanted to learn more about the boys so he pressed on.

"What have you been learning? Do you enjoy any of it?"

Walter spoke up then. "I loved all of it when Miss Cassie was the one teaching." This brought another chuckle from Charles, but he waited for the other boys to chime in.

Tony went into more detail. "All three of us know how to read fairly well. The twins are still learning the bigger words, but they do pretty good. The numbers is where we have a bit more difficulty. We don't really see why we need to know that stuff."

Ross finally made himself heard. "Miss Cassie said there's any number of reasons why we'll need to know how to add and subtract."

Charles responded, "I will have to agree with Miss Cassie. I need to know how to deal with numbers all the time. Mostly to make sure I'm not getting cheated by anyone."

Tony stared at him with an attentive gaze.

Charles continued, "I'll show you the next time we go to the store." This produced three identical grins from the youngsters behind him. Charles laughed again. He hadn't felt this positive in ages. He realized he was grinning back at the boys and tried to return to a more serious mien.

After clearing his throat, Charles commented, "I'm glad to hear you aren't completely averse to going to school. You're all going to need at least a few more years of school."

This did not meet with any enthusiasm but Charles was glad he didn't get much resistance from them either. But then Anton wrinkled his nose. "Didn't you tell Miss Cassie that you needed help on your land? How are we going to help you if we're off at school?"

"Well school isn't every single day, and it's not all year round, so there will be plenty of time for you to lend a hand."

There was silence for a moment while the boys pondered his words. Then Walter piped up with another question.

"How come you don't got a wife, Mister Charles?"

"Have," Charles automatically corrected, shocking himself by it instinctively coming out of his mouth.

"Hunh?" Walter didn't understand.

"You should have asked, how come you don't have a wife," Charles repeated, wondering why he had bothered. This wasn't really the time for a grammar lesson. "Never mind. I don't have a wife because there aren't too many women out here in the wilds of Missouri, and I haven't yet met one that I would consider spending all my days with."

"Miss Cassie isn't married. She'd probably be a good wife," the little boy persisted.

"I think Miss Cassie would be too much work. Besides, she's going back to New York. I don't think she'll stick around these parts much longer than it takes to book a ticket on the next train headed east."

After glancing at the troubled expressions on the boys' faces, Charles realized he should not have said anything less than positive about the youngsters' friend, so he quickly changed the subject.

"We're just about home, boys. You'll have to figure out which bedrooms you'll want to use. We'll get you settled and have our supper. I think a tour of the place will have to wait until tomorrow." This certainly did the job of distracting them. It became apparent they were undecided about the thought of having separate bedrooms.

After exchanging uneasy glances with his brothers, Anton spoke up. "Your house is so big that you have extra rooms?" he asked with surprise.

"Out here there's plenty of space. There's no need to be crammed together like you're probably used to from the city."

"Are you rich?" The boy sounded suspicious.

Charles laughed. "Having a house with more than one bedroom does not necessarily mean a man is rich, Tony."

The boy, despite his rough background, had the grace to realize his question was probably not a polite one, and color could be seen flooding his cheeks. Charles laughed again. "Don't let it trouble you. We're going to be family. I want you to be comfortable to ask me whatever you want."

Tony ducked his head in an awkward nod before getting to the crux of the issue. "We've never slept anywhere but together pretty much since my brothers were born. They probably won't be able to sleep if I'm not with them. And there's only one of me, so maybe it would be better if we still share."

Charles managed to keep from laughing at the boy's serious tone. Of course, he would never admit that he might not be able to bear the separation either. But to spare all of their feelings, Charles merely nodded. "I never thought about how much you'll have to get used to out here since nearly everything will be different than you're used to. Why don't we start out with the three of you sharing the room next to mine, that way I'll be able to hear you if there are any problems in the night. Then, if you change your mind, we can always change it around later."

All he got was solemn silence after his words, so he was glad when, at that moment, they rounded the bend in the road and his homestead could be seen through an opening in the trees. Quiet gasps came from the boys. Charles was a little nervous about their reactions after the conversation they had just had, but when he turned to look at them all he could see was their wide grins.

"I think we're going to like living with you, mister," Ross quietly said as the three brothers stared around with wide eyes, trying to take everything in, even as the light was beginning to fade.

Charles pulled his pair of horses to a standstill near the barn. "We just have to look after these ladies before we head in to get ourselves settled. There's no time like the present for you three to start learning how to look after our animals."

Chapter Four

C assie tried to keep a smile pinned to her face while Katie hovered over her. It wasn't that hard to do, actually, when one considered how funny it must look for the tiny little widow to be trying to hover over her when Cassie was at least half a head taller than Katie. But she appreciated the sentiment behind the actions, so she refrained from laughing.

Gazing at her friend, Cassie shook her head in wonder. "How could you bear to do this trip more than once? I can't believe this is your third time to escort a train full of children away from the city."

Katie's eyes softened as she took in her friend's distress. "I know it's hard to say good bye to the children, but I am absolutely convinced that they will have a far better life out here than they would as gutter snipes in New York. What future would there be for Wally if he had stayed in the city?"

"Oh, I believe you — that's not the issue. I know the boys have a far better chance here than they ever did back home. But how could you bear to part with them?" To her dismay, a tear slid down her cheek as she said those words. She hated to admit to such feelings. Her mother would be aghast at such a display of emotion. But she would have to be made of stone to feel nothing over parting with the dear boys.

"Oh my poor dear," Katie crooned as she pulled Cassie into a warm hug.

Cassie chuckled through her tears. "You can barely reach me and yet you're going to comfort me?"

Katie joined her in laughter and shrugged lightly. "Just because I can barely reach your towering height doesn't mean I can't still offer you a shoulder to cry on."

Cassie laughed again but then pulled herself together. "Morleys don't cry." She offered her friend a soft smile to take the sting out of her rejection of the comfort Katie was offering.

Much to Cassie's regret, Katie looked embarrassed. She quickly rallied and smiled kindly at Cassie. "Morleys may not cry, but I know for a fact that you have a huge heart, and it is perfectly all right to have feelings, you know." There was a slight pause before the older girl continued. "To answer your question, it was far from easy to make any of these trips. And I don't think I can do it anymore. I am actually planning to stay here in Bucklin. There is nothing for me in New York. I need a fresh start. I was working at the orphanage to try to get over the loss I had faced. But as you pointed out, it carries the pain of continual loss, and I don't want to face any more."

Cassie was fascinated with the other woman's decision. "What will you do here?"

"In a town like this, there will be no shortage of opportunities. With an influx of children like this, they will probably need at least one new teacher. The town could probably use a seamstress. The doctor might need an assistant. I doubt I will have trouble finding something to occupy me."

"I have noticed that the male population far outnumbers that of the female. You would have no trouble finding another husband," Cassie pointed out.

"I will never remarry."

Cassie was surprised at the vehemence in Katie's declaration and regretted her statement. She had only been teasing. From what she could see, all the men were much too rough for her taste, so she couldn't blame her friend for not wanting any of them. But she couldn't help her concern and had to point it out to the other woman.

"Don't you think this is a little bit rough of an environment for a woman on her own? Won't you be a little nervous staying here?"

"Cassie, my dear, New York is just as dangerous, perhaps even more so, for a woman on her own. Most of us don't have rich, protective fathers to provide for us."

Cassie felt hot color creeping up her cheeks at her friend's words, no matter how kindly her tone had been. She could no longer meet Katie's gaze. Katie must have regretted what she said as she quickly changed the subject.

"Never mind about me, I have no idea yet what I'm going to do. What about you? Are you going to catch the next train back to New York? I'm pretty sure there's supposed to be another train the day after tomorrow."

With a sigh, Cassie shook her head. She couldn't prevent her frown as she allowed her gaze to sweep over what she could see of the town. "No, despite my discomfort here, I cannot leave yet. The man who was placed in charge of the orphans here does not inspire me with confidence. I have to stay and make sure the children are going to be all right. I know they haven't all yet been placed with families. And I mean to check on all of the ones that have been." When she saw Katie's puzzled expression, she quickly continued, "I feel responsible for them, Katie. I never should have started spending time at the orphanage, but now that I have, I have grown quite fond of the children. And since I made the impulsive choice to come as an escort with the children here to Missouri when one of the others who was supposed to go got sick, I have to make sure they will be well cared for. My conscience would never let me rest if I found out later that they were placed in a bad situation and no one had done anything about it."

"Since I'm staying here, you could leave it with me."

Cassie squeezed her friend's hand. "I know, my dear, but I feel like I need to see with my own eyes that each one is fine. Then I will get myself safely back to my own life. And as soon as I get back to New York, I will find something else to do with my time. I have absolutely no intention of spending any more time with orphans. My weak heart cannot bear it."

"I've always meant to ask you, what ever prompted you to volunteer at the orphanage in the first place? I must say, when you turned up, no one expected you to last longer than the first day."

There was so much truth to the statement that Cassie could not take offense. "The whys and wherefores are a much too long story. We need to be seeing about getting some food for ourselves. I have a sneaky suspicion that tomorrow is going to be a long day."

୫୦ ୧୫

Cassie squinted against the bright sun filling her room. She had slept deeply, her first night in almost two weeks not spent on a train. She hadn't realized quite how tired she had been. But now, feeling fully restored, she regretted not asking to be awakened at an earlier hour. If she wasn't careful, she would allow the day to pass her by with nothing to show for it. She mustn't tarry in this town; it would be hard enough to convince her parents to forgive her as it was. Overstaying in Missouri would surely anger them further.

With that thought, Cassie resolved to visit the telegraph office in order to inform her family that she had arrived safely in Missouri and would be returning shortly. She needn't tell them how long shortly might be. She could see her own wry smile on her face as she glanced in the mirror while she arranged her hair. Getting back to civilization would certainly have its perks, she reminded herself as she lamented her poor skills at styling her hair and wished for her mother's maid to have accompanied her.

She couldn't help chuckling over that thought. Her parents might be upset with her for leaving New York on impulse, but her mother would never have forgiven the breach of taking her maid from her. Cassie's critical eye surveyed her appearance. She was sufficiently satisfied with the efforts the hotel's staff had gone to in order to tidy up her clothes. The worst of the travel wear had been removed, so she was adequately presentable. And she doubted anyone would be able to find fault with her hairstyle. This was far from New York, and no one here knew her or her family. All she really needed was to be clean and tidy. And she could easily manage that without the help of a maid.

Cassie was determined not to be the spoiled rich girl others thought she was. Out here in Missouri, no one knew who the Morleys were, and she rather liked it. Others would judge her for herself, not any preconceived notions. Even if she was only going to be here for a few days, she was determined to make the most of them.

With one last pat to her blonde curls, now under firm control with a multitude of pins, Cassie frowned at her reflection before pinning a neutral smile to her face and sweeping from the small room. First on her agenda would need to be food, she realized as her stomach began to grumble when she caught the smell of baking bread wafting up the stairs. She went down one flight into the saloon. She had been put to the blush the previous night when she had realized that the only accommodation available was over the saloon. Fortunately the owner had appeared to be reasonably respectable. Cassie comforted herself with the realization that no one in New York need ever know where she had slept while away. As long as she was kept safe and warm, she would accept what was on offer. It wouldn't be for too long, she reminded herself once more.

Refusing to dilly dally like a widgeon, Cassie hurried to seat herself at a table. The bartender had promised that there would be food available, and Cassie was starving. Before long she was served. She quickly disposed of the meal and then hurried from the room. Despite it being empty, Cassie could not be comfortable spending any time in what she suspected would be a disreputable place at night.

She was glad that Katie was sharing her room but hadn't heard her leave that morning since she had slept so deeply. Now she realized they would both be pursuing their own interests while here in the town, and she shouldn't feel dismayed that her friend had not waited for her. And were they really friends, anyway? More like acquaintances, Cassie reminded herself with a sniff. All this ridiculous self reflection was going to turn her into a watering pot, she acknowledged to herself with disgust.

Cassie walked briskly, trying to escape the discomfort of her own thoughts. She was hoping to catch the placement manager before he got busy with his day. Cassie wondered how busy the man could possibly be if he hadn't managed to arrange for all the children to have homes organized before they arrived. She reminded herself that she couldn't give in to her indignation. One caught far more flies with honey than with vinegar. In her experience, men were far more likely to accommodate her wishes if she smiled at them than if she frowned. She determined to hold onto her temper no matter the provocation.

She found Mr. McDonald sitting at a dingy desk at the back of the train station. He was leaning back in his chair and had his feet propped up on the edge of his desk, staring off into the middle distance. He didn't seem to notice her approach. Cassie held her breath and counted to ten before she rapped on the door and straightened her smile.

"Good morning, Mr. McDonald," she called as pleasantly as she could manage. His startled reaction made it easier to maintain her smile as genuine amusement flooded her for a moment. And then she once again remembered the children and had to fight to keep her smile in place.

"Miss Morley, what a pleasure to see you this morning." His ingratiating tone lacerated her nerves, but she made an effort to ignore it. "To what do I owe the pleasure of your company?"

"That is kind of you to say, Mr. McDonald. I was just stopping in to see if you had made any progress in placing the last few children." She could see that he was not happy about her question so she batted her eyelashes a little bit, being careful not to roll her eyes, and explained her feelings to him. "It just worries my poor mind and heart what will become of the children if we don't find them a good home."

She must have been convincing because the belligerent look on his face was replaced with a rather smarmy grin. Cassie suppressed her shudder of revulsion and blinked a little more.

"Now you shouldn't be worrying your pretty little head about anything, but I can assure you that I am making every effort to get those boys situated as quickly as possible." He chuckled and winked at her. "You can be sure I don't want them on my hands for any longer than necessary."

"No, of course you don't." She tried to keep her distaste out of her voice. He would at least be motivated now that the children were here since he would be responsible for them until he could find them somewhere to live. Cassie sighed but then managed to turn to him with a smile. "If you need any help, you be sure to let me know."

"But of course, my dear."

Cassie was glad that he seemed to be accepting her interest in the children as natural, so she persisted. "Would it be possible for me to visit with the children while I'm still in town? I'm sure they're feeling a little left out since the other children have already gone to their new homes."

"Well, isn't that sweet of you to be thinking that those orphans have feelings."

She held onto her temper with the last shreds of her self control. "Of course, they have feelings, Mr. McDonald. Just because their parents have died doesn't mean they aren't normal children."

Now it was his turn to blink at her as though he had never even thought such a thing were possible. Cassie wanted to smack the obtuse man but managed to keep a smile pinned to her lips and she batted her eyelashes a little more. She started to wonder if she might perhaps be starting to look like a cow with all the vacuous blinking, but since it was working, she couldn't stop now.

Mr. McDonald looked at her as though he couldn't fathom why she was still there.

Trying not to sigh over how dimwitted he seemed to be, Cassie reminded him gently. "What do you think, Mr. McDonald? If you wouldn't mind, I would like to visit the boys this afternoon, just to try to bolster their spirits, you know?"

"Yes, yes, but of course. You're probably right. Of course they would like to see you. I don't see it to be a problem. I won't be able to be there, seeing as I have to keep working on trying to find them homes, you know?"

"Of course, it is such an important job you have, Mr. McDonald. You must sleep better at night knowing what a service you are performing for these poor children."

The flattery was working like a charm on the incompetent man, and once again, Cassie had to fight not to burst into laughter. Cassie watched in amazement as the man puffed up his chest like a little rooster. Her flattery clearly put him in mind of his duties. Cassie wondered if perhaps he was not as bad as she had thought. Mayhap all the man needed was a little appreciation. She regretted for a moment that she had been insincere in her words until she remembered that incompetence was inexcusable when the children's future was at stake. She maintained her smile, though, hoping that the man's new motivation would hold and he would manage to find homes for all the children before many days had passed. It would have to be disheartening to the ones left behind!

Cassie renewed her determination to visit the youngsters. "Thank you, Mr. McDonald. I know how busy you must be, so I will not keep any more of your time. If you could just point me in the right direction, I will be on my way to see the children."

Within another moment or two she was on her way. Of course, the boys were all happy to see her. Ten of them were squeezed into the inadequate accommodations along with Mrs. Parker and Miss Jones. The two ladies were delighted for additional help in keeping the youngsters occupied. Before long, Cassie had persuaded them all to accompany her out of doors where they wore off some of the boys' excessive energy with a vigorous game of tag.

By the time she took her leave of the group, Cassie was very much in need of tidying and wondered if she should postpone the idea of visiting Walter and his brothers. But those three might be in even more need of her visit than the group had, since they were in unknown surroundings without any adult they were familiar with. After combing some neatness into her curls and washing her face during a brief stop at the hotel above the saloon, Cassie made her way to the smithy to arrange for transportation and directions to Mr. Ainsworth's house.

Cassie wondered if the man could tell she was an excellent horsewoman or if he was trying to get her killed when he walked out of the barn with a huge horse that was tossing his head restlessly. It didn't really matter because she *was* a skilled rider, but it didn't fill her with confidence in the man's reliability. She would have to trust his directions, but she determined to pay attention to her surroundings so she could find her way back to town, just in case she couldn't find Ainsworth's spread.

"You'll be on to his land before you know it, miss. I'm fair to certain he'll be glad for a visit from you." The wiggling of the man's eyebrows did nothing to add to her confidence.

"I am going to check on his children," she replied firmly.

With a shrug, the smithy spat what she could only assume was chewing tobacco, toward a pail not far from her feet. It didn't quite reach the pail but luckily missed her boots. Cassie had to repress a shiver of revulsion. "Anyways once you reach his land you'll still have a good fifteen or twenty minutes of riding before you reach the house. The man bought half the state or thereabouts."

Cassie was surprised at the note of jealousy she heard in the man's voice. She tried to tell herself she didn't care what the man thought of Ainsworth. It only mattered how it might affect the boys, she insisted to herself then decided to ignore the matter all together.

"Thank you for the directions," she replied politely as she stood on the mounting block and climbed onto the huge horse. She allowed her joy at being on horseback to momentarily shake away her concerns as she gave the horse its head and hurried away from the smithy.

Chapter Five

C harles had been momentarily confused when he awoke to the sound of young laughter that morning. Thinking about it as he worked was enough to make him smile. It was definitely something he was looking forward to getting used to. His smile remained in place as he watched the three boys playing in the field. He had been given the impression that they hadn't had very much clean air and open space in their young lives. They hadn't yet talked about it, but he knew there was a great deal of tragedy in their past. There must be; they were orphans after all. But at least they had each other and they were with him now, making a fresh start. He determined once again that he would do his very best to make a good life for them.

His thoughts strayed to Miss Morley, or Miss Cassie, as the boys liked to call her. It had been obvious that she doubted his ability or sincerity in taking on the task of raising the boys without the assistance of a wife. He allowed her doubts to trouble him for a moment. *What if she was right and I won't be able to provide everything the youngsters will need.* He pushed the ridiculous thoughts from his mind. *She was probably concerned about their feelings,* he scoffed, but *if they are to grow into confident men, they needn't concern themselves overmuch about such distractions as feelings, so a woman won't be necessary.* He could provide everything they would need.

Had he conjured her with his thoughts? he wondered almost fancifully before he shook his head for even more foolishness as he watched her approach. It was obvious to Charles that she had a great deal of skill, as he watched her controlling the nearly wild animal the smithy had chosen to lend her. What the man had been thinking to send the young woman off alone with such an ill trained beast, he couldn't imagine, but Miss Morley seemed well able to handle him. She had a wide grin splitting her face, so she obviously didn't mind the effort it had taken to find his property.

Walter and his brothers spotted the lady, and they ran yelling toward her. Their noisy approach upset the horse, and he began to rear. Charles felt his heart lodge in his throat as he took off after the boys, intending to avert disaster.

Miss Morley must have foreseen the trouble. She slid gracefully out of the saddle and had the horse under control before any harm was done, but Charles could not control the rage that rose in him and caused him to lash out at everyone before him.

"How could you be so foolish as to ride this wild animal where there would be children in harm's way?" he demanded of her, his harsh tone ringing louder than usual. "And you boys should never run toward a horse like that! Have you any idea how much damage a large animal like this could do to you?"

All four faces were staring at him with almost identically rounded eyes, shock and dismay displayed equally on each face. Some of the farm hands approached to see what the ruckus was about. Embarrassment piled onto his fright and Charles glared at everyone in equal measure. He couldn't help notice that the young woman was continuing to pat the horse soothingly to prevent him from shying away from his own loud anger.

Feeling his face flush now with embarrassment rather than anger, Charles could not look the young woman in the face. But he felt obligated to apologize to the children. Crouching down on one knee to better reach their level, he put out a beseeching hand. Walter, always the more demonstrative of the three, leaned into him despite the perplexed expression on his face.

"I'm so sorry. I shouldn't have yelled like that. I was doing the exact thing that I was yelling at you for doing. It was not well done of me, and I will try not to let it happen again." He could see that his apology was going a long way to soothing their feelings, but he still had to explain himself. "You have to be careful around any large animal. That horse has not been well trained, but even a well trained horse can be dangerous if it is frightened. He couldn't be sure if you were friendly or not, and the three of you running toward him could have felt like an attack."

"But we were just so excited to see Miss Cassie," Walter pointed out.

"I know, and no doubt she's happy to see you, but you still have to be careful."

The three hung their heads as though they were ashamed of themselves even if they didn't really know what he was talking about. He couldn't bear to think that he had crushed their exuberance and tried to recover from his blunder. "But now you'll know for next time, and there's really no harm done. Nobody got hurt, and Miss Cassie has the beast under control."

He finally made himself look over to where she had taken her mount. Charles was surprised to see that the huge horse appeared docile enough as he drank from the trough and stood beside her quite calmly. Miss Cassie, on the other hand, looked far from calm if you looked her in the eye, but she was doing her best to hide that fact from the children and the horse. She tied the horse's reins in a shady spot and approached the children.

"Now that Hector is under control, I will be very happy to receive the hugs you have ready for me," she told them with a genuine smile on her face. He realized when her focus wasn't on him, she was able to completely hide her displeasure. It was obvious she truly cared about the boys. He tried to amend his first impression of her, but he couldn't manage it. Despite her skill on horseback and her affection for the children, she was a rich, spoiled woman from the city, and she had no business being in Missouri. Knowing who her father was did nothing toward improving his opinion of her. If anything, it made it all the harder for him to tolerate her presence. But despite that, he couldn't help but feel a warm flutter in his midsection whenever he looked at her.

Charles valiantly ignored his feelings of attraction towards the beautiful young Miss Cassie. Despite her appeal, he refused to accept that it was more than skin deep. He would not allow the children's attachment to her to sway his own opinion.

"Where did you get such a huge horse?"

"I didn't know you knew how to ride."

"Did you change your mind and come to stay with us?"

The boys pelted her with questions. Her laughter made his gut clench in a pleasurable fashion, but the last question made his stomach plummet uncomfortably.

He watched as she crouched beside Walter, obviously the one who asked the last question. Cassie kneeled down, seemingly heedless of the dirt to her skirts. It surprised him, but he supposed she could afford to be heedless of her clothes. Since her father was a wealthy cit, he would no doubt just buy her new gowns when she returned home.

But one could not argue that she did not have affection for the boys. Even he was not so cynical as to suppose that her attention to them was feigned. He could not force his gaze away as she drew the small boy into her arms to comfort him.

"No, my dear boy, I am not here to stay. I am here to see where you live. You must show me all the best things about your new home."

Ross and Anton were eager to tell her all about the place.

"And there are ten horses and more cows than we can count and Mr. Charles says we are to each have our own room when we are ready and we're going to go to school just like you said we should."

ℰↄ꒰ᴿ

Cassie couldn't prevent a trill of laughter from escaping her despite the glowering stare of Mr. Charles watching her, like a hawk awaiting its next morsel. The boys really were so dear when they filled her ears with their tales. She tightened her grip on little Wally before releasing him and regaining her feet.

"Now you must show me everything before I have to head back to town. We mustn't tarry, as I do not want to be caught out after dark."

Her words prompted the boys to action. Ross and Walter each grabbed one of her hands, and Anton lead the way. Cassie was uncomfortably conscious of Mr. Ainsworth bringing up the rear without uttering a word.

"Isn't it amazing how much space there is around here, Miss Cassie?" Anton asked her.

"What do you like about that, Tony?" Cassie had wondered if the city dwelling children would be able to adjust to the isolation of Missouri.

"We can't hear the neighbors or smell what they're having to eat. There are birds out here, Miss Cassie."

Ross interrupted with excitement. "And the birds make the prettiest sounds."

"And we saw baby cats, Miss Cassie. Mr. Charles says they're called kittens. He said we can hold them when they get a little bit bigger, but the mama cat won't like it if we touch them now."

They were talking over each other in their eagerness, and Cassie had to bite her lip to prevent tears from forming in her eyes. The poor dears had missed some of the simplest pleasures in life due to their life of poverty. She had known this was a good move for them, but she was even more convinced than ever. Despite how dour Mr. Ainsworth was, she could not suppress the smile of appreciation she cast over her shoulder toward him. The sour man just glowered back at her. She returned her attention to the boys and determined to ignore their new guardian.

"We will be very careful not to disturb the mama, but I would dearly love getting a glimpse of the baby cats, or yes, you are quite correct Walter, kittens. And yes, Tony, I do agree with you, all the birds are lovely, but I cannot decide if I prefer the blue ones or the yellow ones. Which are your favorite?"

"The blue ones, Miss. Although I can see why you would like the yellow ones."

"Are they not the most cheerful color?" she asked.

"They are, but I think the blue ones sound nicer."

They shared a grin.

"You will have to see if you can tame them so that they will come and sit on your finger."

That got all three boys' attention. "Is that even possible?" Ross asked, his eyes wide with eagerness.

She had to shrug. "I would imagine with enough patience and perhaps a bit of bribery with bread crumbs, it would be possible."

Walter and Ross laughed. "We would never have enough patience to sit around and wait for a bird to land on us."

Cassie laughed with them. "No, but Tony might." The boy's eyes lit up at her assessment.

They reached the barn where the cat had nested with her babies.

"Mr. Charles said we have to be very quiet." Wally's whisper was the loudest she had ever heard, but Cassie managed not to giggle as they tiptoed through the large building, past the empty stalls to the last one, where it was dark, warm, and quiet. A mound of hay was piled up in front of the stall door, all the better for the youngsters to be able to peer over its edge. Cassie found she could not detest the dour man, who had still not said anything. If he was so thoughtful toward her boys, she would not judge him for seeming so stern. It was obvious he must have a kind heart despite his severe exterior. Or perhaps he did not like women. She chose to ignore his gruffness and think well of him. All thoughts of the grouchy man were pushed to the back of her mind as she joined the children in their delighted examination of the mother cat with her babies.

The boys couldn't stand still watching for very long. When she realized they were beginning to fidget and would soon make the cat anxious, she drew them away with a tap on their shoulders and a beckoning gesture.

"There are too many other things to see before I leave," she reminded them when they were a little away from the last stall.

"You'll come back again, though, right, Miss Cassie?" Walter worried.

"Of course, my dear. You will soon grow weary of my visits."

"Never," he declared with determined loyalty.

Cassie laughed, taking his hand again and following Tony and Ross as they continued their tour of the property.

"We haven't seen everything yet. Mr. Charles says we have to learn to ride before he can show us all over the place."

"Oh, have I interrupted your opportunity for riding lessons?" she asked with dismay. "But I would love to watch. Do not, I pray you, allow my presence to prevent you." She turned toward Ainsworth as she spoke.

"But you still haven't been in to see the boys' rooms." Ainsworth finally spoke. Cassie wasn't sure if he didn't want to give the boys' their lesson while she was there or if he was trying to prevent the necessity of her returning. She ignored either possibility.

"That can wait until next time, I'm sure. Perhaps I could be of assistance with the riding lessons so that the boys needn't take turns. They could learn all the faster that way."

She had thought she was being reasonable, but he merely looked annoyed. She ignored his reaction and turned back to the boys.

"You are going to love riding! It is the best feeling."

"But are you not afraid being so far off the ground?" Walter asked, his nerves evident.

"Not if your saddle has been adjusted properly and you have firm control of your mount. And I am most certain that Mr. Ainsworth will be very careful in his selection of which horses he shares with you. You can be sure they will be gentle and dependable. There will be nothing to fear."

"I'm not afraid," Tony boasted while Ross chimed in. "Me neither."

Walter looked up at her with pleading eyes. Cassie squeezed his hand reassuringly but said nothing else. It was a skill the boy would require living out here on such a large property and so far from town. He could only walk so far on his little legs. She was delighted she would be there to share the treat of helping her young friends learn.

An hour or two later, she had lost all track of time, she was exhausted from all the laughter she and the boys had shared. Mr. Ainsworth had barely thawed toward her and so had not shared in most of their laughter, but Cassie was relieved to see that he was not so stern with the boys despite the scowl that creased his face continually.

Despite the fact that the boys had barely even seen horses in their young lives, Cassie was heartened to see they had an aptitude for riding and it would soon seem as though they had been born in the saddle. Even Walter was beginning to enjoy the activity, she was relieved to see. Glancing at the location of the sun, she bit back a gasp of alarm.

"Oh dear, I really must be off or I will lose myself in the dark on the way back to town. I had no intention of staying this long."

There was a chorus of protests from the boys, but she hugged them all in a hurry and promised to return as soon as she could manage. She hadn't felt particularly welcomed by their new guardian so she didn't want to promise to return the very next day. She would have to give the matter a little more thought before she braved his presence again.

She was gazing at the stirrup in dismay, wondering if there was a mounting block handy when Ainsworth actually laughed. The sound startled her into glancing in his direction for the first time in at least an hour. She had been ignoring him as steadfastly as she could manage. The man discomfited her. But when he laughed she felt a flutter in the region she was pretty sure housed her heart, which made her frown. He really was distractingly handsome even when he scowled. But when he smiled, his appeal was almost overwhelming. She couldn't help smiling in return.

Without saying a word, he cupped his hands, silently offering to hoist her up onto her horse. She was uncomfortable placing herself so close to him, but admonished herself not to be a ninny. There was very little other choice, and she really needed to be on her way. Taking a deep breath, she drew close to him, placed one foot in his hands and clambered up onto the horse with as much grace and dignity as she could muster, quickly settling her skirts and hoping she did not appear anywhere near as flustered as she felt.

"It really was much easier to give them their first riding lesson with you here. Maybe you could come back tomorrow and we could try again." His low voice sent a shiver up her spine, while his words nearly robbed her of speech.

The stern man was inviting her back? Wonders would never cease it would seem. She hoped her face was not flaming as she felt a myriad of feelings assailing her.

Without answering him, she called out to the boys a goodbye and wheeled her horse around. "I really must be off. Farewell," she said as she goaded her horse into a trot. She left the yard in a small cloud of dust. She realized that was probably quite rude of her. She wasn't used to the dirt like there was around here; in the city everything was cobbled or at least oiled. But as her horse progressed to a cantor and then a gallop, she allowed the wind whipping by her to blow away her concerns, at least for a few minutes.

Chapter Six

When she pried her eyes open the next morning, Cassie was dismayed to see she had again slept later than she had planned. She was being far more active than she was used to, and it was making her need more sleep. She hurried to ready herself and set out for more visits with the children. She intended to return to Ainsworth's property to see Walter and his brothers after she made stops with some of the other children who had been placed. While the three brothers held a bigger piece of her heart, she felt compelled to check on all of them before she returned home to New York.

The prospect of getting back on the train held no appeal for her at the moment, so she shoved the thought away and concentrated on the instructions the smithy was giving her on how to arrive at her first destination. He gave her a vague warning about being careful out on her own, but since all the places she was going were reasonably close to town, she chose to ignore him. He made her slightly uncomfortable. She couldn't decide if the smithy was being helpful or suggestive.

She crisscrossed the remote scenery, vaguely admiring the rugged beauty, but her attention was focused on ensuring she didn't get lost, while her thoughts were occupied with the children she left behind at each stop and the ones she would see at the next. More and more convinced that she could no longer volunteer with orphans, Cassie wondered what she was going to do with her life after this venture was concluded.

With a sigh of relief, she saw Mr. Ainsworth's house come into view. She had saved the best for last, she thought with a frisson of misgiving as she remembered the cold reception she had received from Ainsworth the day before. She shoved that thought from her mind as she concentrated on her joy at seeing her favorite boys again.

Cassie was dismayed at how quiet the property seemed when she approached the house. She wasn't really surprised by the depth of her disappointment. She knew she would have to leave Missouri sooner rather than later and wanted to spend as much time as possible with her favorite trio before she returned to New York.

She had never realized she would get so attached to the children when she had signed up to volunteer at the orphanage. She didn't know how she was going to live without them when she left, but she knew for a fact that she couldn't handle going back to the orphanage. Her heart couldn't take the losses.

Feeling melancholy, she sat atop her rented horse, gazing about at the beautiful prospect, reflecting how different it was from the city, when she was startled by an exuberant shout from behind her. Within minutes, she was off her mount and surrounded by the three youngsters who were again all talking over each other, each wanting to tell her everything that had happened since the previous afternoon.

"Mr. Charles has arranged for us to have all the clothes we could possibly need."

"We're going to start going to school in a couple days."

"He says if we don't start soon we'll be too far behind."

"There was so much food, Miss Cassie, we couldn't even finish it all."

Cassie had to laugh. This last statement was said with such reverence, and then all three boys grew silent as though this was too overwhelming to even contemplate. It wasn't really a laughing matter that the poor boys had experienced hunger, but the alternative was to cry and they wouldn't have appreciated that.

"It certainly sounds like you are being well provided for," she observed as she made herself meet Mr. Ainsworth's gaze. "Thank you for that, sir."

He offered her a half shrug and a lopsided grin, as though he were uncomfortable with her weak praise. It heartened Cassie to see his reaction. It seemed obvious to her that he had not taken on the boys in an attempt to curry favor with someone. Unlike the socialites of New York. Including her. Cassie was ashamed of her early attitude and was very conscious of others' motivations. Despite his off-putting demeanor, Cassie was determined to try to think better of Mr. Ainsworth. She offered him a brilliant smile but then had to fight not to laugh when suspicion crossed his face.

"Are you going to help us with our riding lessons again today, Miss Cassie? We waited, hoping you would come."

"Mr. Charles didn't think you would and said we ought to go ahead without you, but we knew you would be here."

Cassie's feelings of appreciation for Mr. Charles slipped slightly when she heard these words, but she forced herself to remain polite even though she could no longer look at him.

She squeezed Walter's hand. "I'm glad you had confidence in me, dear boy. Of course, I'm here for your riding lesson. We had such fun yesterday, I couldn't bear to miss out today. Thank you for waiting for me. I'm sure it wasn't easy for you."

As she was talking, they began to walk toward the barn.

"Why did you look sad when you were waiting for us, Miss Cassie?"

Cassie was surprised by Tony's question. The children had rarely expressed any notice of the feelings of the adults around them.

"I thought I had missed you. It seemed so quiet when I rode into the yard, so I was sad that I wasn't going to get to see you today. Then you came running out to greet me and I was happy again."

"I wish we could see you every day for always." This from Walter, and Cassie had to blink to keep the tears from her eyes.

"I know, but we'll always be friends. Once you know how to write really well you could write letters to me, and I will be happy to stay in touch with you."

The boys didn't look convinced. "But that won't be the same as seeing you."

"No, but it's better than nothing," she answered as briskly as she could manage. "Let's not think about it now. I'm going to stay around for a little while longer. Let's make the most of the time we have."

Walter still lacked a little enthusiasm, but the three boys ran ahead of her to get the horses ready for their lesson.

Charles came up beside her. Cassie was uncomfortable around him but tried not to show it. She offered him a tentative smile.

"They're such sweet boys," she began before she had to clear her throat because of the wobble in her voice. "They sure have become captivated with what you're doing for them here. I'm glad to see how quickly they're adapting. They're going to have a great life here with you."

She could feel tears forming in her eyes and was quick to blink them away. She didn't figure the grumpy man would appreciate her softer side.

✺✧

Charles watched as she nervously licked her lips and blinked back the tears that had formed on her eyelashes. He wondered if she was trying to gain his sympathy. It was a tactic he had seen girls try before, but he had no interest in hard-hearted women who were into manipulation. He knew what girls like her were like, and he wanted none of it.

But he knew the boys were fond of her, so he would tolerate her presence for as long as she stayed in town in order to provide them with a sense of continuity. Even though he wasn't inclined to like her, he had to admit she had handled the youngsters' concerns quite well. Even though he expected the New York socialite to be a flighty little thing, he grudgingly admitted that he could learn a thing or two from her about dealing with the boys.

"Was this your family's land, Mr. Ainsworth? Have you lived here all your life?"

He never appreciated anyone asking him questions about his past. "No," he answered her simply, trying to keep the anger out of his voice as he said it. He must not have been completely successful, he realized, when she turned her startled gaze up to meet his eyes.

"I apologize, Mr. Ainsworth, if my questions were impertinent, I was merely curious. But my mother has, on occasion, informed me that curiosity is vulgar. It would seem she was correct." She offered him a tight smile that he did not return. He did not want to be friends with her. She deftly changed the subject. "What will we be teaching the children today?"

Once again, the afternoon passed quickly. Charles was surprised by how much he enjoyed teaching the boys. They were so receptive and eager. And he had to admit that Miss Morley was of great assistance. Now all the youngsters needed was practice, to reinforce what they had learned.

"Will you come back very soon, Miss Cassie, and go for a ride with us?" Ross asked.

"Yes, please come." Walter added his plea.

"Mr. Charles said he would show us more of his spread once we knew how to ride. You would probably like to see it too, wouldn't you?" Tony asked. His shy smile revealed how much he hoped the young woman would join them.

Charles couldn't resist the boys' wishes. He added his invitation to theirs. "It would probably be good if you came too,

Miss Morley. I think they need one more day of practice, and then we can plan for a longer ride. It would make it easier for me to lead the way if I knew you were bringing up the rear, keeping an eye on the boys' riding progress. Then I would only need one hand to come along to watch for any dangers."

He shouldn't have added that last bit, as he was met with four pairs of rounded eyes. "What kind of dangers?" Cassie asked for all of them while obviously trying not to look too scared.

"There are any number of things we need to be concerned about. I won't go into too much detail at the moment. You needn't worry. My men and I will keep you safe."

He could tell she didn't appreciate not being told what she wanted to know. He found her good looking whatever she was doing, but when she was irritated and trying to hide that fact, he found it particularly endearing. It was unlikely she would appreciate his thoughts. He ignored the pull of attraction. She was too pretty and soft for the life he was living here. It didn't matter if he thought she was the most beautiful woman he had ever laid eyes on, she was not for him, and it would be well for him to remember that.

Charles watched as Walter grabbed Miss Morley's hand. "You'll still come, though, right, Miss Cassie? Mr. Charles said you don't need to be scared."

He watched as she blinked at the boy and then smiled widely at him. Crouching down beside him, she looked the boy in the eyes. "Of course, we needn't be afraid. I am quite certain Mr. Ainsworth is capable of keeping us safe. I wouldn't miss it for anything."

Charles was pretty sure she had to force herself to look at him. "You are planning for the day after tomorrow, right? That works well for me as I have a few things I ought to take care of in the meantime. What time would you like me to arrive for our ride, Mr. Ainsworth?" Her tone was polite and cool. The perfect voice for a New York socialite, he thought in derision, ignoring the pull in his belly at the sound of it.

"If you could come at eleven, that will leave us enough daylight to go for a nice long ride and you would still have time to make it back to town before dusk. Perhaps we could even eat our lunch at the back of the property by the river."

She nodded briskly and turned back to the boys. "Then I will see you all at eleven o'clock, day after tomorrow. Make sure you don't leave without me."

The three boys clamored to hug her goodbye while insisting they would never leave her behind. Charles gritted his teeth, ignoring his jealousy over their attachment to the young woman. He had always thought children were good judges of character, but now he wasn't so sure. He wouldn't trust this woman farther than he could throw her, but the children would give their lives for her, he was sure. He was glad she would soon be returning to New York. Since the boys loved her, he couldn't deny her access to them, but he didn't want her around any longer than necessary. He would ask her tomorrow which train she planned to take.

Charles almost smiled as he watched Walter, Ross, and Anton talking over each other and Cassie gamely trying to keep track of what each of them was saying while they walked toward her horse. They came to stand with him as she rode away. Walter's hand made its way into his grasp. Charles was still a little uncomfortable with such displays but didn't want to hurt his feelings so allowed it for a moment. His heart went out to the little boy. Charles knew he was going to love being a father.

"Why do you s'pose Miss Cassie doesn't want to stay here with us, Mr. Charles? Maybe you could adopt her, too." Ross' six-year-old logic left a little to be desired, Charles thought as he wondered how to answer him. Thankfully Ross' big brother stepped in.

"Don't be stupid, Ross. She still has her parents, so she can't be adopted."

"But I don't want her to go away." Ross' voice trembled, and Charles' heart clenched in sympathy.

"What do you like about Miss Cassie, Ross?" Charles asked. "Maybe there are some ladies around here you could be friends with."

The boy shook his head. "It wouldn't be the same, Mr. Charles. Miss Cassie knew us before. It's different, you know."

Charles didn't know, but he couldn't argue with the boy.

"I like that she always listens," Walter piped up.

"And remembers," Ross added. Charles' confusion must have been evident because Ross elaborated. "Grownups often pretend to listen to what you say but don't remember what you told them. Miss Cassie always listens *and* remembers."

"And then she asks you about it, like to check on you," Anton chimed in. "Like if you had a loose tooth or had been planning to play a game, she would ask you how did it go."

Charles was surprised by their words. "I can see why you would appreciate qualities like that."

Walter summed up how all the boys felt. "The other ladies that were at the orphanage, and especially the ones who came on the train with us, are nice, but Miss Cassie is the best."

"I'm sure she would appreciate knowing you feel that way," was all Charles could say before he changed the subject. "Now, who would like some dinner? I don't know about you three, but I sure did work up an appetite today."

"Me!" "Me!" "I do, too." They were easily distracted, and the evening drifted to a comfortable close.

Chapter Seven

C assie was less than comfortable sitting in the saloon eating her supper. If her parents could see her, they would lock her up and throw away the key, she thought with reluctant amusement. They were going to be less than pleased with her for going on this trip in the first place, even if they never found out what her accommodations were like.

She tried not to draw any attention to herself and ate as quickly as possible. It was still early, so the bar wasn't crowded, but Cassie was well aware that the men of the town were unused to having a proper woman in their presence while they were drinking. But she had been far too hungry after leaving her mount at the smithy and couldn't wait to eat until morning. She would have no strength for her ride tomorrow if she skipped supper tonight.

It was one more reason why she needed to make up her mind to buy a ticket back to New York. She knew Kate and Melanie, two of the other women who had accompanied the orphans on the train, were planning to stay in town and had already arranged for a place to live. Katie had only shared her room in the hotel that first night. She and Mel had quickly found a more permanent accommodation. Perhaps she could see if they had a little bit of room for her to stay with them for a couple more days. She just couldn't tear herself away from the children. She doubted it was going to get any easier as the time went on, but she just had to be sure all the children from the train were looked after. Maybe she would buy the ticket once Mr. McDonald had finished placing them all. She knew she wouldn't be able to have a clear conscience until that was looked after.

As soon as she finished her last bite, she signalled to the bartender and hurried up the stairs to her room. She was sure to get indigestion from how quickly she had eaten, but she couldn't be comfortable with all the attention focused on her.

Once she got to her room, she contemplated her plans for the next day. She resolved to visit Mr. McDonald again to see if he had made any progress. She would speak with Kate and Melanie as well, to see if they would mind her staying with them. Cassie would happily pay them what the hotel was charging her. She knew they were both needing to take on work as soon as possible, so they must not have very much money. And it was only fair that she contribute. She would just be glad to be away from the saloon.

She managed to drift off to sleep despite the rising volume from the men in the bar. All the riding and fresh air were certainly making for deep sleep, she thought vaguely as her exhaustion finally swallowed her. She thought of nothing else until the sun streaming through her window woke her early the next morning. She was glad to see that she had managed to be up at an early enough hour this time. She could not spend another night above the saloon!

After quickly dressing and gathering together her few things, she made her way downstairs. The saloon was empty except for the ever present bartender. Cassie wondered if the poor man ever slept. He offered to make her breakfast, for which she was grateful. Before the large clock struck the hour she was on her way.

Deciding first to speak with Mr. McDonald just in case the man was going to leave his office that day, Cassie headed toward the train station, as his office was next door.

"Miss Morley, what a pleasure to see you this morning." The fat man's friendly greeting was surprising.

Cassie smiled. "Thank you, Mr. McDonald. How are you on this fine day?"

"I am well, my dear, I am well." His exuberance was making her nervous for a reason she couldn't quite define. "You will be happy to hear that I have now found a place for all but two of the orphans you brought with you. And I am fairly certain that the last ones should be placed before the week is out. I just have to make one more visit to confirm with someone who had expressed an interest previously."

"That is wonderful news. Are you confident the children will be happy where you've placed them, sir?"

Cassie winced when she saw how the man reacted to her question and quickly tried to disarm him. "I apologize, sir, I have no intention of questioning your abilities. I just find that I am so worried about the poor children. You know how it is, don't you?" It wasn't hard to make tears gather in her eyes. She truly was worried for them, especially with their fates being left in the incompetent hands of this uncaring lout.

Her words had the desired effect. No longer looking mulish, Mr. McDonald patted her awkwardly on her shoulder. "Of course I understand. Don't get yourself in a taking, young lady. I have every confidence that I am finding good homes for each and every one of those orphans. Anywhere out here is going to be a far cry better than where they come from, wouldn't you agree, Miss Morley?"

No, I do not agree, she thought with fierce anger that she made every effort to hide. What she said out loud was far different. "I am certain they are all happy to be getting settled into families once again. Would you be so kind as to give me the direction of the children that have now found a good home? I wouldn't want to leave town without saying goodbye."

"Of course, of course." He was back to being jovial, no doubt relieved that she wasn't going to give in to a fit of the vapors and glad to have a reason to send her off.

Within moments she had the paper with all the names clutched in her hand and she was on her way from his office heading away from the train station toward the small house Kate and Melanie were renting.

"Cassie! What a pleasure to see you! What has been keeping you so busy that we haven't laid eyes on you in the last couple of days?" Kate's welcome was warm but censorious.

"You look as though you have settled in already. It has only been a couple days, but I'm sorry if you were expecting me earlier. I have been junketing about the area checking on the children. I don't trust that Mr. McDonald was particularly interested in the welfare of the children when he made the arrangements. I could not leave here with a clear conscience if I did not see with my own eyes that the children were content with their new homes."

Kate nodded in sympathy. "Oh, you poor thing. You haven't managed this experience very well, have you? Of course, I understand. That's one more reason I'm glad that I'll be staying here. I will be able to lend a hand if any of the boys find themselves in need of a little assistance." Kate smiled warmly and turned the subject. "Please say you can stay for a little visit. I have just put the kettle on. Say you'll have a cup of tea with me."

"That would be lovely, thank you. I just left Mr. McDonald and could use a cup of tea to put a better taste in my mouth."

The two young women shared a chuckle. Cassie glanced around the small but comfortable space.

"This is a lovely home you have, Kate. I can see that you're already happy here."

"Yes. Having a fresh start is wonderful. I'm sure there will be a few things that I will miss from the city, but I never would have been able to have a home like this there. It was all I could manage to afford a small room in an ugly tenement."

Cassie, being from far different circumstances, became a little uncomfortable, but happy for her friend. She turned the subject. "Is Melanie home?"

"No, she is out considering her options. Since I have already been promised the position of schoolteacher, she is looking about to see what her employment prospects are. She is highly skilled with a needle, so she is thinking she might be able to be a seamstress. There is already a tailor in town, so she has gone to speak with him. Perhaps he can refer her to some clients, or she could assist him."

"I do hope it works out for her," Cassie answered as she nodded her thanks for the piping hot cup of tea Katie placed before her.

"How long do you expect to stick around, Cassie? I thought you would have caught the train back to New York that went through this morning."

Cassie shook her head. "I know my family will no doubt be furious. I didn't even get a letter ready to send on the train to them. Do you know if there is a telegraph office? I hadn't thought to check yet. I have just been so occupied with worry over the boys."

Soft-hearted Katie grasped her friend's hand. "What are you going to do, Cassie? You have become far too attached to these children. There is very little you can do for them."

Cassie appreciated her friend's concern but she refused to accept her words. "Perhaps little, but not nothing." She softened her hard words with a smile. "The good news is, so far, the children that I have visited in their new homes are happy with their new arrangements. For the most part, the families who have taken them in are kind and delighted to expand their families. From what I can see, it's a tough, lonely life out on these large spreads, and the couples who have taken in some of the boys are happy to have more people at their table."

"Have you seen Walter and his brothers?" Kate asked with a hesitant tone.

Cassie nodded. "While I found Mr. Ainsworth to be a grumpy, even cold, man, the boys have quite taken to him. I worry that he won't understand their struggles as they deal with all that they've lost in their young lives, but he certainly seems to have the ability to provide for them well in a material way. His house is quite large and he has many animals and extensive gardens. The boys were commenting how much food there has been at each meal." Cassie's laugh was a little strained as she and Kate shared a glance.

"It will be better for them here, you know that," Kate reminded her.

"I do know that, as long as they are with kind people. That's all I ask. I could not bear it if any of the children were placed with someone who will mistreat them, Katie." She paused for a moment and Kate merely waited for her to continue. "I saw Mr. McDonald this morning. He kept calling them orphans. I know that's what the children are, since they have lost both parents, but the way he said it was as though that made them lesser creatures. It was all I could do to remain civil with the man, but I had to because I fear he will be even more incompetent if I upset him in some way."

They both sighed before Katie spoke up. "It is a cruel and unjust world. Mr. Brace's idea is a sound one, but in reality, it's only as good as those implementing it. But as you observed, most people are good and decent and will provide a satisfactory home for the children, which is far better than they had living on the streets of New York."

Cassie's smile was fraying, but she tried to hold onto her composure as she met her friend's eyes. "I know. In reality, I never should have volunteered at the orphanage in the first place. I don't think it will do the children any good to see me going to pieces over saying goodbye to them. But I cannot leave town until I am convinced that they will all be well. I know I don't have much power, but I have a little, and I will use it in whatever way I can to ensure that they will be well after I leave."

"You have a good heart, my friend," Katie said.

"No, I don't," Cassie countered, amused when she saw how surprised Kate was over her words. "My motives have never been completely pure in connection with the orphanage. And now, I am not fully convinced that my concern for the boys is purely for their sake or for my own. I don't want to have to live with a guilty conscience over them."

Katie let out a peel of laughter. "Well, even if your motivation is merely to keep your conscience clear, the fact that it would bother your conscience says something good about you."

Cassie joined her in chuckling before she got to the point of her visit. "Either way, I find that I cannot yet leave this town, but the hotel is unacceptable." She glanced around the small space. "I know it would be an imposition, but do you think I could possibly stay..."

Kate did not allow her to finish asking. "Of course you must stay here! I am so sorry that I didn't think of it myself. I thought you might be more comfortable at the hotel and that you would only be a night or two anyway."

"It is certainly not your fault, my dear Kate. But no, the hotel is not a fit place for me to stay, and since I can't leave for at least a couple more days, I need to make other arrangements."

"Well, just bring your things over here. We don't have much, but you are welcome to it anyhow."

"Thank you so much. It's kind of you to say. I know I'll be imposing and I will try not to stay too long."

Kate interrupted again. "It's never an imposition to make room for a friend. You are welcome to stay as long as you need." She gestured around. "This might not be much space compared to what you're used to, but for me and Melanie it's grand, so we won't mind sharing and you can have a room to yourself. You'll have to excuse the simplicity. The place came furnished, thankfully, but it has been empty for a while and in need of a little attention."

"That's generous of you, Katie. After living on the train for almost two weeks, I too am thinking that any space bigger than a train car is grand, so I don't mind sharing either. But since you have said yes, I will gratefully take whatever you offer." With a grin she got to her feet. "Now, I will hurry back to the hotel and get my things. I have promised Walter, Ross, and Tony that I would go riding with them this afternoon and am due there at two, so I ought to hurry."

"Would you like me to come with you to lend a hand?"

"You are too kind, Katie, but no, I will hire a boy to carry my trunk, which is really all I have."

"Of course," was all Katie said in answer, making Cassie wonder if she should have accepted her offer of help. She bit her lip but decided not to take back her words. There was really no way to undo what had already been said, and if she accepted Katie's help, she would have to carry the other side of the heavy trunk, and it would take them twice as long. With a silent sigh, Cassie swallowed her regret that she could never quite fit in and hurried back to the hotel.

After enduring another uncomfortable encounter at the saloon and then arranging for her trunk to be taken to Katie's house, Cassie stopped in at the general store, grateful to see that it was surprisingly well stocked. She picked up a few food items that she thought Katie and Melanie might appreciate. Cassie wasn't sure, on second thought, if she should offer them any money for staying with them, but she was sure they would be glad to have her contribute some food. Cassie knew neither of the other women would have a great deal of savings, and especially until Melanie found work, they would need to stretch their money as far as possible. It was the least she could do, since they were saving her from the indignity of the saloon.

෨෬

"I am so grateful for you taking me in like this, Katie! A man who had been frequenting the saloon tried to follow me up to my room when I returned for my things. Thankfully the bartender noticed and stopped him, but it made me nervous and uncomfortable. I wouldn't have been able to sleep a wink if I was staying there tonight."

Katie made soothing noises as she bustled around getting things settled for Cassie. "You poor thing! We should have thought to ask you to stay with us from the beginning. I apologize, Cassie."

"Don't be silly. How were you to know?" Cassie was embarrassed to have made her friend uncomfortable. She briskly changed the subject. "Now, what can I do to help you be more settled? You mentioned earlier that there were still things to be done."

"Oh no, Cassie, we couldn't ask you to help with that," Katie protested. "All that is left is washing some walls. It can keep until later."

Cassie laughed. "You mean until after I've ceased imposing upon you? You absolutely must allow me to wash some walls. I made arrangements to have this afternoon to do whatever I could to help you and Melanie here, and I mean to do it to my best ability. I became quite a good wall washer on the train ride here, so you saved the perfect assignment for me."

Katie tried to protest a little more, but Cassie could tell it was half-hearted. She was glad there was something specific she could help the other women with. It didn't sit comfortably with her to accept their kindness without trying to return some of it.

"What do you mean you made arrangements?" Katie thought to ask.

"Ainsworth has said I may accompany them as he rides out through his property to show it to the boys. I asked that it be tomorrow, as I was hoping you would allow me to come stay here with you."

"Were the boys disappointed to hear you wouldn't be coming today?"

"Of course," Cassie replied on a laugh. "But it's better for them, I think, to have one more day of practicing their riding before we go out for a longer trek. According to the smithy, Mr. Ainsworth owns a great deal of property, so I'm anticipating that it will be quite a lengthy ride."

By this time, the efficient Katie had stowed Cassie's things in one of the bedrooms and had procured a bucket full of warm water and several cloths. She wrinkled her nose at Cassie. "Are you absolutely sure you want to do this? I promise you, I will not hold any ill feelings toward you if you decided you aren't up to it."

Cassie laughed then sighed. "I fear you have a similar opinion of me as does Mr. Ainsworth. I swear to you, I may have been a debutante back in New York City, but I have learned to be quite proficient with a damp cloth."

Katie trilled with laughter. "Very well. Let us have at it." She handed Cassie a cloth, and the two of them began scrubbing the walls in the main room. "But don't think you can get away without explaining yourself. What do you mean that you are proficient with a cloth? And it seems to me that you're protesting Mr. Ainsworth's opinion a little too much. He is a terribly handsome man…" She trailed off with a giggle, and Cassie could feel heat climbing in her cheeks.

Cassie tried to brazen through the other woman's words by focusing on her first question. "Didn't you find it horrifically filthy on the train with all the smoke everywhere? I couldn't bear to think of the boys breathing in all that soot through the night, so I took to washing the walls most days. I thought everyone was doing it." She could feel the heat in her cheeks intensifying at Katie's incredulous stare.

Katie laughed a little as she replied. "Unfortunately, most of us have gotten too used to grime. In many parts of the city back home, there was similar smoke at times. Maybe not as bad as on the train, but more than I suppose you would have been used to. So no, I can assure you, most of us did not wash the train walls daily."

Cassie couldn't help but laugh at Katie's words. "Well, I guess my sheltered life did a little bit of good for the children, then. And it was a good lesson for me." After their laughter died down, a comfortable silence settled between them, and they made rapid progress around the small room.

"You weren't joking when you said you were proficient with a damp cloth," Katie commented at one point, making Cassie beam with pride.

There were a few more moments of quiet before Katie giggled and stated," You never did tell me about Mr. Ainsworth. I'm getting more and more curious, you must realize."

Cassie sighed and protested, "There's nothing to be curious about. I can assure you! The man always seems to be cross about something and thinks little of my presence. He has yelled at me, glared at me, and usually only offers me silence. I do not think he approves of the boys' affection for me." This flabbergasted Cassie, but Katie didn't comment so Cassie continued. "Perhaps he is just jealous of how close I am with the boys and is being defensive without even realizing it. But I don't really think it's that. It seems to me as though he took one look at me on the very first day we were in Bucklin and found me wanting. He can probably tell from looking at me that I am nothing more than a socialite and has deemed me beneath his notice. But he hasn't even given me a chance to prove there is more to me than that. He merely judged me from what he can see on the surface."

She barely registered how furiously she was scrubbing the walls as she continued her complaints about the man. "I think he has been too good looking all his life and is used to everyone thinking him superior for it. It's hardly an attractive quality, in my opinion. I try to keep my eyes averted when I'm there," she confided with a small giggle. "Looking at him is far too distracting and can make one forget how grumpy he seems to be."

"Is he grumpy toward the boys?" Katie worried.

"Not usually. He seems to save it for me. Except for the time I arrived on a half wild horse and the boys ran toward me. He let all of us have the rough side of his tongue over that, let me tell you." She paused as she thought. "But it might have been prompted by fear that the children were going to get hurt."

"If he's saving his grumpy side for you, it could be because is trying to cover up warmer feelings he might have toward you."

"Katie Carter! What are you getting on about? You have declared that you have no interest in marriage. Why are you suddenly playing matchmaker?"

Katie didn't seem to take offense at Cassie's scolding. She shrugged. "Just because *I* don't want a husband doesn't mean I don't think anyone else should have one. I have never heard you make any declarations about wishing to remain a spinster."

Cassie could feel herself begin to splutter. "Well, no, of course not. I have no intention of remaining a spinster. It is just that I cannot marry a man who would consider I have nothing to offer him."

Katie frowned over her choice of words.

"In New York, if I marry someone from my own circles, I will bring value with me. My name, my father's connections, my social experience will all be of value to a prospective husband."

"Oh Cassie, surely you realize you are of far more value than your father's name."

Now it was Cassie's turn to shrug. "Not really. I don't have much in the way of useful skills. Being out here shows me that all the more clearly. I can't make clothes like you and Melanie can. I don't know how to cook very many things. I know nothing about animals."

Katie interrupted Cassie's stream of self deprecation. "But you know how to make people smile. You can usually read people very well. And the children love you. Every single one of them. You are a bright young woman. Everything can be learned if you know how to use your mind. And I've seen you use your mind to accomplish whatever you set your mind to. Remember that time you came with me to the market for the orphanage? I couldn't believe how nice the produce was that we managed to buy. And the butcher gave us a far superior cut of beef than he would have given me, just because you asked the right questions and batted your eyelashes at the right time."

Cassie laughed. "That was such fun."

"See what I mean? You didn't even mind doing it. You are far braver than I am. Mr. Ainsworth would be lucky to have you."

Cassie laughed again. "While he would be lovely to look at, I am not convinced we would be the best match."

Katie merely hummed and cast her a knowing glance. There was nothing Cassie could do but laugh again. She didn't want to add fuel to Katie's exclamation that she was protesting too much. Cassie wondered if there was a chance Katie was right. She thought of the taciturn cowboy with a smile but quickly shook her head and returned to her task.

Within a couple hours they had washed every wall in the small house and returned it to a tidy state. Cassie felt as though her arms had turned to the consistency of oatmeal, but she also felt a deep sense of satisfaction from their labors.

"Cassie, thank you ever so much. I would not have had the motivation to get all this done at once without your help and company. It is such a relief to have it done. And it feels so clean and fresh in here. Our home will be a true pleasure to return to." Katie's gratitude warmed Cassie's heart but embarrassed her a little bit, too.

"No thanks necessary, I assure you. I am just relieved that I could be of real help since you have been so kind as to take me in. I feel a little like the orphans we have brought out here."

"Not at all," Melanie, who had since returned home, insisted. "You are our friend. We're glad to have you with us. But all the more so since you were so generous as to help with this onerous job. The treats you brought us from the mercantile would have been enough." When Cassie shook her head, Melanie continued. "Don't shake your head at us. Allow us to appreciate what you have done. I know you aren't used to doing this type of thing. So you probably also aren't used to genuine gratitude. Accept it."

With a shared laugh, the three young women sat down to rest from their day. Cassie couldn't keep the grin off her face. She was certain it was the most sore she had ever felt in her entire life, but she was also certain that it was the most content she had ever felt as well. She rather thought she would like to extend her time here in Missouri to enjoy these friendships a little longer.

The next morning, Cassie bustled around helping Katie a little bit before making her way to the smithy once more after promising to be back before dark. Katie had laughed with her when Cassie had assured her that Ainsworth's grumpy behavior would surely have her returning before too long.

"You ought to just buy yourself a horse, Miss. It don't make no sense for you to be renting every day," the smithy pointed out.

"I'm not going to be staying in town much longer. Besides, I haven't anywhere to keep a horse."

"You could board him here during your stay and sell him before you leave."

Cassie thought over his words as she rode toward the Ainsworth property. She knew he was only being reasonable from his own standpoint, but since she didn't know how long she would be staying, she didn't want to commit herself to owning a horse. Then she thought of another thing. She should have checked at the train station for the eastbound schedule over the next week or two so that she would have an idea of when she should be planning to head home. And she really needed to send a message to her family. They would be ready to skin her alive by the time she got home, she thought uneasily before she allowed the worries to get blown away as she urged her horse into a gallop.

She arrived at the ranch with time to spare. Again it appeared quiet when she rode up. After tying her reins to a fence, she walked up to the front door of Mr. Ainsworth's house. Before she even had a chance to knock, the door was flung open by an exuberant Walter, who threw himself into her arms.

"Miss Cassie, you made it!"

"Of course, I did," she answered with a grin as she set him back on his feet after a tight hug. "But I think I'm a little bit early. Are you boys in the middle of something?"

"We were just doing some school work. Mr. Charles wants to see what we know before he sends us to school."

"That's wonderful, Walter. But you don't sound too happy about it."

"I would ever so much rather be out in the barn."

"I know you would, but never mind about that. We are going to have a wonderful afternoon of riding." She smiled as the other boys came to join them. "I'm sorry that I have interrupted you. Hurry and finish up while I wait out on the porch. I wouldn't want Mr. Ainsworth to think I am interfering with your studies."

The boys laughed as though she had been joking, but Cassie was truly concerned that the austere man would curtail any future visits if he suspected she would interrupt their learning. She smiled at them, not wanting to interfere with their relationship with their new guardian and let herself back out of the house.

A few minutes later a gruff voice made her jump.

"What are you doing out here by yourself?"

She had been staring out into the sunny landscape, lost in thought, and hadn't noticed his approach. With a hand on her pounding heart, she turned her head toward Mr. Ainsworth.

"Good heavens, you nearly frightened a year off my life."

He scowled at her words. "You should be paying more attention. This isn't the city. You need to keep your wits about you."

Cassie tried to pull her dignity around her. "After the first couple of days at the hotel, I cannot say I completely disagree with you, but I would think the city would require more attention than out here. There is a pickpocket around every corner in New York. Out here you can ride for miles without encountering a single person."

"It's not necessarily people you need to be concerned about in these parts," was his cryptic answer before he continued. "But never mind that, why are you out here by yourself? You should have let me know you had arrived."

Cassie shrugged. "I got here earlier than we had arranged. When I arrived, the boys were still involved in the assignment you had left for them, and I didn't want to disrupt their work. I'm good enough company to keep myself occupied until our appointed time."

She had thought she was being genial, but he only grunted in reply. Cassie stifled her sigh but kept a smile on her lips.

"If I had realized you were here, we could have gotten on the way earlier." His surly attitude put Cassie's teeth on edge but she refused to rise to his bait. She was determined to enjoy the afternoon with her favorite boys.

Cassie shrugged again. "Well, now you know, so we can be on our way." She forced herself to smile at him, not wanting the boys, who had just come out of the house at the sound of their voices, to see them arguing. Even though she didn't like the grouchy Mr. Ainsworth, she could not undermine the boys' respect for him or interfere with the relationship they were building together. Despite his unmistakable antipathy toward her, it was obvious that he was kind to the children and they were beginning to care for him. She started to frown as she thought about how confusing the man's behaviour was but then caught Walter's watchful gaze on her and smoothed out the crease that had formed on her forehead. She offered him a warm smile, and he came and took her hand.

Within a few moments, they were all saddled up and on their way.

The grass was so tall in some places that it was hitting her boots where they hung in the stirrups. It was probably an odd thing to notice, but it really struck Cassie as she took in her surroundings. She had been so preoccupied as she rode around visiting the boys and dealing with her mixture of emotions that she had barely registered the scenery around her. That all changed as they rode just for the sake of getting to know the land.

Back in the city, everything was so groomed and controlled. She couldn't quite decide if she found the wilderness beautiful, but it was certainly exhilarating. It made her want to goad her horse into going faster. It made her want to scream and laugh and take the pins out of her hair so it could stream wildly down her back. Clearly it made her run mad.

She glanced back at Mr. Ainsworth. Cassie knew there was no way he could read her thoughts, but she felt the compulsion to check anyway. Of course, as usual, his face was inscrutable. It frustrated her that she couldn't tell what he was thinking. But at least he wasn't falling off his horse laughing at her. Not that she should care what he thought of her, she reminded herself. The handsome man was not for her, she insisted to her heart.

Maybe she just really needed to get back to the city. She would never have thought trees and grass and a wide, blue sky would be at all appealing to her, but she quite liked being able to see all around her. It gave her a sense of security that did not exist in the crowded avenues of the city. But the city was so much more genteel than this rugged wilderness. Her dithering thoughts were driving her mad.

Not that it really matters anyway, she mused and allowed her gaze to follow the meanderings of a bird as it flitted along beside them. It wasn't as though she were considering staying here. In Bucklin, Missouri, of all places. She would be disowned for sure. Even if she had an employable skill, she didn't think she could stay no matter how attached she was to the boys. She was a New York socialite, and she needed to return to the life she knew. So maybe she ought to simply enjoy the beautiful surroundings instead of questioning why she was enjoying it so much.

ॐ ও

Charles struggled to keep his attention focused on watching for dangers as they rode near the boundary of his property. His eyes kept straying toward the blonde beauty talking animatedly with his new sons. He felt his chest puff up with pride over the thought that he was now a father. He would be the first to admit that he hadn't even considered being a parent until the nearby town had started to buzz with the news of the incoming orphans. But when he had heard about them, he couldn't rid himself of thoughts of the poor youngsters and what he could do for them.

Now that he had the three of them, he already couldn't imagine his life without them. But their attachment to Miss Morley was a problem he would have to deal with before long, since it would seem she wasn't in any hurry to leave town. He only wished he didn't find her quite so attractive. He reminded himself once more that it was merely surface-deep beauty. *A socialite from New York couldn't possibly have any noble qualities*, he insisted to himself. Perhaps if he talked to her, he could rid himself of this ridiculous attraction.

He guided his horse into position next to hers with practiced skill. She appeared startled by his sudden nearness. Charles ignored his instinctive pride over her obvious awareness of him. It shouldn't matter a jot whether or not she found him attractive; he certainly had every intention of overlooking any attraction he felt toward her. He was sure it would be made all the more easy if he talked to her.

"You must be finding it difficult being away from the city for so long. When will you be catching the train back to New York?"

She turned her head to look at him, a frown marring her forehead. "Are you trying to get rid of me, Mr. Ainsworth?" She laughed as she said it, but he could see the seriousness in her eyes. He wanted to ignore the obvious intelligence stamped on her face. It was easier to consider her nothing more than a silly socialite. What was even harder to ignore was the increased pace of his heartbeat when in her presence. He needed to focus on the matter at hand.

He remembered her question and shook his head. "Of course not, Miss Morley, I was merely wondering what your plans are."

He could hear the sarcasm dripping from her reply. "It's kind of you to be concerned for me, but you needn't trouble yourself. I am not feeling the loss of the city overly. I shall survive the deprivation a little while longer. I haven't decided when I will be returning."

"Your parents won't be too pleased about that."

She offered a small shrug and kept her focus on the trail ahead. "That needn't concern you."

Charles clenched his teeth over her attitude. "As a new father, I can tell you that if one of my sons was far away, I would be very concerned about his whereabouts."

She grinned at him, and he ground his teeth together. "I'm so happy to hear that you are becoming so protective of the boys." She paused as she once again turned her focus ahead of her. "I am sure my parents are anxious to hear from me. They will be furious with me for leaving town. And I will probably be locked in my room as soon as I return so that I can never leave again."

He was incredulous. "Did your parents not know you were coming to Missouri?"

Again she shrugged. "They would have forbidden it if I had asked."

Charles was appalled at her callous attitude toward their feelings. "Do they know where you are now?"

"Yes, I sent them a message at the first stop the train made. They would never have understood my need to make sure the children were safe."

"Why are those three boys so important to you that you would do that to your own family?"

"It wasn't just Walter, Ross, and Anton that I was concerned about. I needed to see that they were all going to be well cared for. But I do have a particular fondness for your sons," she concluded with a soft smile.

Charles couldn't see past the fact that she had left her family to worry about her. "I don't think I want you around my boys anymore, Miss Morley. I would never want them to show such disregard for my feelings as you have for the feelings of your parents. You are not a good companion for them. You need to go back to New York and let them get on with their lives."

The look she turned on him was filled with reproach. "You don't know what you are talking about when it comes to my family, and I will leave when I'm good and ready to leave. I am most definitely not a bad associate for your sons, who, I will remind you, I know better than you do. You have already given your promise that I can spend as much time as possible with them before I return to New York. I am sure they will not take kindly to you trying to curtail that."

His already clenched jaw began to ache from his frustration. He felt as though she were extorting from him. And she was right. The boys would not thank him for removing her from them. They so obviously loved her. He wanted to ignore her but decided further conversation might help him get over his anger with her. His feelings were so divided. It was driving him mad. He didn't want to be attracted to her, but he couldn't seem to help himself. With a quiet sigh, he probed a little more.

"How did you get involved with the orphans in the first place? It doesn't really strike me as being in keeping with your position."

She looked puzzled over his word choices but offered him a polite smile. It was apparent she was happy to move on to some other topic rather than discussing her appalling treatment of her family.

"I don't think you really know my position, sir, but you are correct in saying that it wouldn't have been my first choice, and I have no intention of continuing at the orphanage when I return to the city. I cannot bear the losses. It is too easy to fall in love with the children, but being involved with the orphanage made me much too aware of the challenges that unfortunate people face, and there is far too little that I can do to help. It breaks my heart." He watched in fascination as she swallowed back the threat of tears. It was the most emotion she had ever displayed in front of him. "I am unsure what I will do with my time when I return to the city. My family will want me to marry, of course, and start a family of my own." Her gaze was trained on the boys ahead of them. "I am not opposed to the thought, but it is difficult to find a suitable mate, and I don't want to settle for merely acceptable."

He frowned with confusion over her words, but before he could ask her for clarification she continued on. "In answer to your question about how I got involved with the orphanage, I am ashamed to say it was not with noble intention. I had managed to get a reputation as being vain and spoiled, and it was suggested that I ought to do some volunteer work to improve my image."

"Why would a girl like you need to improve her image?"

"Apparently very few eligible men are looking for over indulged young women to be their wives." She shrugged again as though it really didn't bother her, but Charles couldn't decide how genuine her feelings were. "My parents wanted me to do something more genteel like sewing things for needy families, but I wanted to be more involved than that. They were not most pleased by my choice, but they were probably right in their assessment. I was too spoiled to care for their reaction. They were convinced I would catch some dread disease from the children. But nothing of the sort took place. And then I no longer cared about my reputation, I grew to love everyone at the orphanage and spent as much time there as possible, even though most of my friends turned their noses up at the thought of me being in that part of town." Cassie shrugged again, almost helplessly. "I really don't know what I'm going to do when I go back. I can probably join some committee raising funds for the needy. But it just doesn't feel the same as actually helping them with my own hands." She glanced down at her hands as they held the reins. "Of course, my mother would have apoplexy if she saw the state that my hands are in. I shall have to be sure to buy some salve before I leave town, and hopefully the ride back will give them time to be restored." She grinned and offered yet another shrug. "Or I will just have to make sure I wear gloves whenever I am in my mother's presence."

Now he was curious. "Why are your hands in a poor state?" He was growing fascinated with watching the girl talk. Myriads of emotions flitted across her face as she spoke. He couldn't identify most of them, but he was beginning to suspect she wasn't as depthless as he had thought. This wasn't helping him find her less attractive, but for the moment, he couldn't convince himself to mind.

Now she looked sheepish. "It started on the train. Thankfully there was no shortage of water, so I was able to keep things clean for the children. I cannot think the soot from the train is healthy for them to breathe. So I had to regularly wash the walls and their blankets. My hands were unused to such exposure. At least at the orphanage we have tools and equipment to assist. Then I helped my friends clean their new place here in town. They are going to allow me to stay with them until I return to New York, so helping them was really the least I could do."

Charles blinked, unsure how to reply or if a reply was even necessary. The young woman didn't look as though she were expecting him to say anything, but he felt as though he ought to. But to hear her say that she had been washing the children's walls and bedding with her bare hands left him a little speechless. He couldn't fathom a Morley of New York doing such a thing. He grinned.

"I don't think you need to worry about your mother. She would never believe that you would do something so menial as chores. She will no doubt blame the weather conditions in such a desolate place as Missouri."

His stomach clenched as she released a tinkle of laughter over his words. "You are probably right, Mr. Ainsworth. Thank you for that comforting thought. I may just face my parents' wrath for avoiding my latest suitor for so long."

Surprised by a surge of what could only be jealousy, Charles gazed at her, hoping his mouth wasn't hanging open. "Have you left a gentleman in the lurch while you are here?"

She frowned at him and searched his face, obviously trying to divine the intentions behind his question. "Of course not. Not that it is any of your business, Mr. Ainsworth, but I would never leave anyone in the lurch if I could help it."

"Not even your parents?" he pursued, although he questioned his own intentions at this point.

She immediately became defensive. "I swear to you, I sent them a telegraph at the very first stop the train made. I'm certain they were notified of my whereabouts before they would have even realized I was gone. I did not leave them to wonder about me." She had the grace to blush. She paused before continuing a little more softly. "My parents' expectations are impossible for me to live up to. They want me to replicate their lives with my own."

"Would that be so terrible?"

She huffed a breath and appeared frustrated. "Not if I wanted the same life as they have. Then it would probably be quite lovely. But I don't. Want their life, that is. The type of gentleman they wish for me to marry is no longer the type I can see myself spending my life with."

He wanted to ask her more about that but suddenly remembered she had mentioned something about trouble at the hotel. "What did you mean when you said you could understand about trouble coming from people in these parts?"

She looked confused by his question so he prompted her, "Remember, earlier, when you had just arrived, and I was displeased that you were outside by yourself. I said you needed to keep your wits about you. You argued that New York was less safe, but you didn't seem to completely disagree with me. Did something happen to you at the hotel?"

He was fascinated but troubled by the blush climbing her cheeks.

"I handled the situation and will no longer be staying there, so it needn't concern you."

Little did she know, he thought, her words made him all the more concerned, rather than alleviating any worry. He tried to resist the protective feelings building in his chest but feared he was not as successful as he would wish.

Much to his relief, she turned to him suddenly, changing the subject. "Have you ever been to New York, Mr. Ainsworth?"

"I have," he answered reluctantly, wondering where she was going with this question. He wasn't going to find out, though, because they were suddenly interrupted by Ross calling to them.

"You two need to hurry up. We're never going to get there."

With a laugh full of joy, the woman beside him spurred her horse into a faster gait and left him behind, watching after her with doubts filling his mind. She was not exactly how he had thought she was. In fact, if he allowed himself to dwell on it, he was probably going to start thinking she was pretty great. That just would not do, so he shoved such thoughts to the back of his head. There was no way he could be attracted to a Morley socialite from New York city! He too urged his mount to a faster pace and quickly caught up with the others — the boys were laughing and once again vying for Miss Morley's attention.

Chapter Eight

The boys' chatter helped distract Cassie's mind from the conversation she had been having with Mr. Ainsworth. It rattled her to realize how hurt she was by his obvious judgment of her. She couldn't help who her family was, and she made every effort not to be like them. She was reasonably certain she was no longer anything like them, in fact. But Mr. Ainsworth had judged her nonetheless. Frustration simmered in her chest, but with a slight huff she pushed the restless thoughts from her mind and focused her attention on the boys' chatter.

"And then the kittens licked me and I laughed so hard I almost fell out of the haymow and Mr. Charles said I wasn't allowed up there anymore." Ross' mixture of joy and dismay was almost palpable and made Cassie's heart constrict with the desire to hold onto the young boy and never let him go.

"Well, the good news is, the kittens will probably soon be big enough to leave the haymow, so you won't be separated for long."

Ross shrugged, trying not to look upset. "Yeah, that's what Mr. Charles said." He looked at her with wide, eager eyes. "But what if he's wrong? What if they forget me in the meantime?"

Cassie almost choked on her own gasp. She had the exact same concern about the boys. *What if they forget me after I'm gone?* Pasting what she hoped was a reassuring smile to her face, Cassie wished she was on the ground so she could hug the small boy. Instead she said, "I'm sure if you love them enough they'll remember you no matter what." When he still didn't look convinced, she continued. "Even if she does, you can get reacquainted as soon as she leaves the hay, can't you?"

This, at least, the boy could accept. They were quickly interrupted by the other boys, and the conversation flowed away from the touchy subject. But Cassie's heart still felt achy after those thoughts. It took some effort to keep a smile on her face and to pay attention to the boys' banter. Despite her melancholy, they soon had her captivated once more.

She was a little surprised when Tony urged his horse as close as he could manage to hers. Glancing over at him, she could see he was eager to speak without being overheard. She had to stifle her grin. She so loved these boys, she thought; her heart felt as though it was swelling in her chest. Cassie was quite certain the boy's furtive glances were not going unnoticed by anyone, but she managed not to make eye contact with anyone else and thus succeeded in holding back her laughter.

"It's not very interesting around here, is it?" Tony whispered.

Cassie wasn't sure what she had thought the boy had wanted to discuss with her, but this certainly wasn't it. She could no longer hold onto her amusement and a quickly stifled laugh erupted from her. His disgruntled glower helped her get her amusement under control.

Looking around, she assumed the boy meant the scenery since the three youngsters had not ceased talking about all that had captivated them on Mr. Ainsworth's ranch. They were following a trail that had been worn into the landscape, although Cassie wouldn't be able to tell why they were following it. As far as the eye could see there wasn't a single building, just gently rolling, grass-covered hills, with a few trees dotting the landscape. The lushness of the greenery told Cassie that it was most likely very productive soil, and she was sure Mr. Ainsworth was successful in his agricultural endeavors. But she could imagine that would not interest the city-bred boy overmuch.

"Why are you whispering?" she needed to ask.

"I don't want to insult Mr. Charles," he answered as a dull blush crept into his cheeks.

Cassie had to bite her lip to prevent her laughter from returning. "I don't think he'll take it personally, Tony. I think it will just take a bit of time for you to get used to the scenery around here."

"But what if I don't get used to it? What if I'm completely bored?"

The poor boy seemed genuinely concerned. All trace of laughter left Cassie as her heart went out to him. "You are a smart boy, Tony. While it's true that life out here is going to be very different from your life in New York, that doesn't mean it will be boring. There are so many new things you will have to learn about your new home, especially if you're going to help Mr. Ainsworth with his animals and land. I don't think there will be a shortage of things to do. And while it will take longer to get to school or to visit your neighbors, at least you will get to ride a horse in order to get there."

The boy grinned at that. "That's true. That will be great."

"And you can run and jump and play with your brothers so much better here than in the city, since there is so much more space. There won't be anyone yelling at you or the chance that you'll get run over by a passing carriage, either."

He was nodding slowly, listening closely to her words. She continued, "I think you will come to love it out here. Most of the other children that arrived on the train with us are near enough that you might even go to the same school with many of them, so you will have plenty of opportunity to stay in contact with them."

"I hadn't even thought of that. That will be good. Walter and Ross will be particularly happy about that, I think." He paused, thinking the matter over some more. "I guess you're right, Miss Cassie. It probably won't be boring once we get used to being country mice." They exchanged grins before he sobered again and added, "But you won't be here, so there will still be something missing."

Tears welled in her eyes and she had to look away so the boy wouldn't see. At first she was staring sightlessly off into the middle distance, but then motion caught her attention. Blinking away her tears, her eyes focused on what she was seeing.

On a small rise, not that far away, three men on horseback were watching them. A shiver of apprehension shimmied up her spine. They did not strike her as fine, upstanding citizens. She would have thought that in such a sparsely populated area, if one encountered others, they would at least wave, but the three men seemed to be scowling at them. They put her in mind of some of the more unsavory characters that she had had to watch out for around the orphanage back in the city. She wondered if they had followed them here. She turned to Mr. Ainsworth and was just about to ask him about them when he spoke up before she could say anything.

₧₧

"Let's turn off here and head down to the river. The horses could use a drink, and it will be a good place for us to have our lunch."

Charles had to concentrate so as not to squirm under her searching gaze. In that moment, he wished Miss Morley was the simple-minded socialite he had been convinced she was, but it was obvious to him that she was far from stupid, even if she was shallow. He watched as her gaze flicked between his face and the three ruffians watching their group. Then she glanced at the boys, and a smile bloomed on her face. It seemed to him that it wasn't as natural as usual, but he was glad when she began talking.

"Oh, I do look forward to seeing the river. I am quite certain my poor horse is nearly parched."

"Why do you think that, Miss Cassie?" Walter asked predictably.

"Well, I'm very thirsty myself, and I haven't had to carry anyone around all morning."

Her droll tone drew laughter from the boys and even the ranch hands that were accompanying them. Charles felt his lips tip up in the corners in appreciation of her quick thinking, but he was too preoccupied with his own concerns to join in the conversation. He was surprised, though, to realize how reassuring he found her voice as she carried on conversation with the boys.

"Have you been to the river before, Ross?" She was always so careful to involve all three boys in most conversations.

"Not yet, Miss Cassie. Mr. Charles has been quite busy since we got here, and we haven't been on any long rides before today," Ross explained.

Tony interrupted. "It wasn't just 'cause he was busy, remember? He said we would be too sore if we went too far before we got used to riding."

"Well that was very thoughtful of Mr. Charles, wasn't it? I'm sure he's right. I've been quite used to riding, but after sitting on the train for so long I got out of practice and I felt it after my first day on a horse once we got here, let me tell you. Since you lads have never ridden before now, it is good that you work up to it."

The youngsters were listening to her as though she were an oracle, he thought sourly. He ought to be grateful that she wasn't contradicting him. He should even be glad that she was complimenting him. But it wasn't to his face, he acknowledged before returning his attention to watching for danger. He WAS glad that she was keeping the boys occupied, but her chatter was a distraction to him and he had to concentrate to maintain his focus, as part of his mind enjoyed listening to her conversation.

"Do you find that you like riding on horses, now that you are a little more used to it?"

This was met with resounding enthusiasm.

"Absolutely!"

"It's the best!"

"Yes!"

All three answers came simultaneously, resulting in her rich laughter ringing out. "Well I am certainly glad of that. You would be in a fine mess if you didn't like to ride."

There was a pause. The boys were still laughing, but Charles felt her assessing gaze flicker towards him again. He hoped his expression was as bland as he was trying to make it. He didn't meet her eye, so he wasn't sure how convincing he was. It didn't matter. She resumed her chatter with the boys.

"Did you name your horses or did they have names already?"

"They already had names, and Mr. Charles said they know their own names so it would confuse them if we tried to call them something else."

"That makes sense, doesn't it? You would probably think it was really strange if Mr. Charles started calling you something other than your names, right?"

"I guess so," Walter answered.

"You still sound disappointed," she pointed out. "What name did you want to give your horse?"

"Scout," came his quick reply.

"That sounds like a good name for a horse," she answered. "Maybe you can just save it until you get a chance to get a young horse that doesn't have a name yet."

"That's what Mr. Charles said. He said we can name all the animals that get born on his property from now on, but we have to take turns."

"That sounds very generous of him. I'm sure the three of you will have a great time naming all the animals as they come along."

She paused for a moment before asking, "Do you think Mr. Charles knows how grateful you are that he is letting you use his horses and he is taking his time to teach you so many things?"

This earned her puzzled glances from all three boys before they all glanced back at Charles with sheepish faces. Charles was sure they were hoping he wasn't listening to the conversation. He tried to remain impassive but the urge to laugh was strong. He was glad when they quickly shifted their focus back to her.

Tony spoke up. "He might not realize it since I just realized it myself."

"That's alright, Tony. Now that you know, you'll remember to tell him next time he does something nice for you, I'm sure. It seems to me that he has done plenty for you. People usually appreciate hearing thank you once in a while."

Charles was curious how long she was going to drag that out but was surprised when she allowed the matter to drop. Of course, what the boys said next could have caught her attention.

"See, Miss Cassie, this is why you should stay here with us. How will we know about things like this without you here to teach us?" Tony was obviously trying to sound reasonable, but his tone shifted to wheedling.

Miss Morley laughed, although to Charles it sounded more forced than usual. "You boys will do just fine with or without me."

"But don't you want to stay with us, Miss Cassie?" Walter asked.

"Of course I do, Walter, but that's not how it works."

"You could have the extra bedroom, Miss Cassie," Ross offered. "Mr. Charles said it's for when we get comfortable and want our own rooms, but me and Walter can share and you could have it."

"That is kind of you to offer, Ross, but Mr. Charles hasn't invited me to stay." The boys looked as though they were about to protest, so she carried on. "Even if he did, it would not be appropriate for me to live with a bunch of boys and a man, don't you think?"

"Maybe you could marry Mr. Charles," Walter interjected eagerly. "Then you could be our mother."

Tony wrinkled his nose. "I don't think Miss Cassie is old enough to be our mother."

Walter was not to be dissuaded so easily. "Well, if she married Mr. Charles, she would be our family anyway. Mr. Charles said he's our family now, even if he isn't our father. So she would be our family, too, and could stay with us forever."

Charles could hear every word of the conversation and was trying not to fidget in his saddle. He fervently hoped the woman came up with a suitable reply, although he couldn't fathom what it would be. He was relieved to hear her tinkle of laughter.

"Oh, I do love you three so much! Thank you for wanting to keep me with you. I never want to leave you, either, but I don't know if I can make a life for myself here in Missouri. Maybe I could in Kansas City, but not here in Bucklin. There isn't much for a person like me to do in these parts."

Tony spoke up. "You think we can learn to like it here, don't you?"

The young woman blushed as she realized where the youngster was going with his question. "Yes, I do. And I suppose you're going to say that I could learn to like it, too, aren't you?"

The boy grinned and nodded eagerly.

"The thing is, whether or not I could learn to like it isn't the issue. My life is back there in New York."

"We had a life there, too," Tony answered quietly.

She must have been feeling desperate because she finally looked at Charles as though searching for help. Charles wasn't sure what was written on his face, but she must have realized he didn't have the answer because she turned back to the boys.

"For one thing, the three of you still have each other, and you are here all together so it isn't the same thing." When they were going to protest further, she quickly continued with a small laugh that sounded forced. "Never mind about it now. I promise that I will give it more thought later. But for now, I am famished, and if my ears are not deceiving me I am almost certain that we have reached the river Mr. Ainsworth promised us. Let us get down and give our horses a rest."

Charles watched as she deftly managed to turn the children's attention away from the uncomfortable conversation. A part of him was offended that she had not coquettishly tried to gain his approval of the boys' suggestion. But another part was grateful that she had handled it so deftly and he wasn't left to explain to the boys why he didn't want their beloved Miss Cassie in a bedroom down the hall from him. He ignored the part that thought the boys' suggestion had merit.

While they ate, Charles kept his attention divided between watching for the men who had been observing them and listening to the boys chatter with Miss Cassie. The hands who had accompanied them had taken their own lunch and spread out to stand guard further away. So far it would seem that they had not been followed.

He thought back to what the boys had asked her. She was perfectly correct, there was nothing for her here in the wilds of Missouri. The type of women needed here were tough, experienced women, trained in something more useful than how to entertain. A New York socialite wouldn't survive through the first winter on the plains, let alone the lonely realities of life on the frontier. Just because she was beautiful and the boys loved her didn't give him any right to even consider keeping her here.

The rest of the day passed without event, but he could feel Cassie's watchful gaze touching on him from time to time. He was rather sure that she had noticed the three men and wanted to ask him about them. Charles was surprised by her restraint.

Chapter Nine

C assie woke up with a dull ache in her heart that spread to her stomach. She had barely been able to eat the delectable breakfast that Katie had prepared that morning. She had grown closer to Katie and Mel in the few weeks since they'd left New York than she had with any of the friends she had grown up with, and she was dreading saying good bye to them. It amazed her how attached she was growing to everyone she was coming into contact with in this remote part of the world. Perhaps it was the very remoteness that made each relationship so special, she pondered as she rode out of the town once more. She had just one more house to visit. The last of the orphans from the train had been placed and she needed to see for herself that they were well.

The solitary ride to the small farm where Liam and Henry now lived was peaceful, and Cassie was surprised by how much she enjoyed the fresh air and quiet. She had begun to see the beauty in what had previously seemed monotonous and dull to her city bred senses. Realizing she was on the verge of turning melancholy, Cassie entertained herself for the rest of her ride with thoughts of what she would do with her time once she returned home. Unfortunately, all of her previous pursuits now struck her as shallow except for her time spent at the orphanage, but she had vowed to herself that she could no longer volunteer with orphans. With a sigh, she realized she would have to discover new things to do with her time. Perhaps she could become a teacher, she thought. Getting a little more education for herself would keep her occupied when she first returned to the city, and then being in a classroom would allow her to spend time with children but keep her from growing overly attached. Thus resolved, she set her chin resolutely just as she arrived at the Smiths' farm.

"G'day, Miss Morely," the homely older woman greeted after Cassie knocked on the door. "Won't you come in and have a cup of tea? We don't often get visitors."

"Thank you, Mrs. Smith. I must apologize for stopping in unannounced, but when I heard that you had taken Liam and Henry, I just had to stop in and congratulate them on their new home."

Mrs. Smith blushed timidly over Cassie's words and fluttered nervously around her kitchen. "We were lucky to get them. We were late finding out about the trainload of children and were worried we were too late when we finally got into town to see about them. Mr. Smith and I haven't yet been blessed with children of our own, so being able to take two such healthy boys in is a godsend for us. They are so polite and eager to learn, I can hardly believe they hadn't been claimed yet."

While the older woman had been talking, Cassie had taken the seat she had indicated at the table and glanced around as surreptitiously as she could manage, pleased to see that while the home was humble, it was neat and clean. And she was delighted to see several books on a low shelf. While all of the families who took in the orphans were expected to ensure the children received an education, Cassie had no idea how that could be enforced. Seeing books in the home made her feel that learning might not be considered trivial to the farming family, which raised the Smiths higher in Cassie's estimation.

Mrs. Smith had just placed a steaming cup of tea in front of her and a small plate of cookies on the table when there was a commotion at the door.

"Miss Cassie!" chorused two young voices followed by a deeper, more restrained greeting of "Miss Morley" from Mr. Smith.

Cassie stood to greet the three male arrivals. Four arms quickly encircled her.

"You came to visit us, Miss Cassie," Liam declared with glee. "Did you know we have a new home?"

"Yes, I heard and just had to come in person to congratulate you."

Henry squeezed her tight before letting her go. "There are cows and chickens and I haven't been hungry once since we left New York, Miss Cassie."

Cassie had to blink hard and swallow the lump forming in her throat before she could answer him. "I'm delighted to hear it. And I brought a little something for each of you as a welcome home present."

"You did?" Liam asked as he exchanged a glance with Henry.

"What is it?" Henry demanded.

They were so excited to open the small packages. Cassie felt as though her cheeks were burning from the grin splitting her face. It was such a relief for her to see their happiness. The gifts were small and had cost her little, but the boys had probably never received gifts for themselves. Their eyes were glowing as they opened the bag of marbles and the box of quoits. They couldn't wait to try them out.

As the boys headed out to play and Cassie turned back to her cooling tea, Mrs. Smith smiled warmly at her. "That was mighty kind of you, Miss Morley, I thank you deeply. We don't have much, but we're going to try our best to give these boys a good life."

"I can see that, Mrs. Smith, and I am so happy for it. I have grown attached to all the children we came out here with and I haven't been able to rest easy until I knew that they have all found decent homes. Seeing you with them has taken a weight off my mind."

"It will be our pleasure to maintain that," the older woman answered with dignity. "If you would like, we can correspond occasionally so you can keep up with their development."

Tears once again welled in Cassie's eyes. "I would like that above all things, thank you."

After a little more conversation, Cassie stood to take her leave. "I shouldn't keep you from your day much longer. Thank you for taking the time to let me visit and see how lucky Liam and Henry are to have been found by you."

Mrs. Smith appeared gratified by Cassie's words but waved them away. "We are the lucky ones. They are bright, healthy, and eager boys. It will be our privilege and duty to guide them into fine young men."

Cassie rode away from the Smith farm with deeply conflicted feelings. She was relieved beyond belief that the last of the children had found a good home. She had been worried that Liam and Henry wouldn't find a good placement. They weren't related to each other, but had grown close and would be wonderful brothers to each other in their new home. She could tell that while the Smiths may not have a lot to offer materially, they were prepared to give them love and attention, which would benefit them more than gold.

But now there was nothing holding her in Bucklin. She had no more excuses to stick around. It was time to buy her ticket back to New York. And say her goodbyes to Walter, Ross, and Tony. She urged her horse to a faster gait as she turned towards the Ainsworth spread.

From a distance she could see an unusual amount of activity in the yard. As she drew even closer, she was shocked to see Ross sitting on the front porch stairs, crying. She jumped down from her horse before it had even come to a complete stop and ran toward him.

"What has happened? Are you hurt?" she felt frantic but tried to keep the panic from her voice.

Ross's tearstained face was tragic. "We can't find Walter. I think he ran away."

Putting her arms around the young boy, Cassie sat down on the step beside him and tried to stem his tears. "Tell me what happened," she said in a low, soothing voice.

Ross snuggled into her arms with a shuddering sob. "While we were eating breakfast, Walter was pestering Mr. Charles to ask you to stay with us. When Mr. Charles told him that you don't belong here and you need to go back to New York, Walter told him he hates him and that he would go find you himself and get you to take him with you. But since you're here without him, I guess he didn't find you."

"Oh no! No, I haven't seen him. What happened next? Is that the last you've seen of him?"

Ross nodded and sniffled. "Bob from the barn said Walter tried to saddle his horse but he wouldn't let him so he ran out behind the barn."

"Why didn't Bob stop him?" Cassie was horrified.

Ross shrugged. "He didn't think anything of it, I guess. And he was busy with his chores."

Cassie was rubbing circles on Ross's back and his crying had slowly subsided to shuddering breaths. She pulled a handkerchief from her pocket and wiped his face. "Don't worry, Ross, he couldn't have gone too far. I'm sure we'll be able to find him before long. He has probably just found a nice spot for a good sulk and he'll come out when he's good and ready."

"Do you really think so?" His small voice sounded so hopeful.

"Sure I do. Walter is a smart boy. He'll realize he won't be able to find me, even if he had a horse, let alone on foot." She stood up and held her hand out for Ross to grab. "Now, let's go find Mr. Charles and see what we should do."

As Ross took her hand, the loud clearing of a throat behind her made Cassie jump, and hot color flooded her face. Mr. Ainsworth was about ten paces away and watching her intently. He looked as though he had heard every word she said but doubted her sanity. He also looked furious with her.

"Have you seen him?" he demanded.

She blinked. "Walter, do you mean?"

"Yes, have you seen him? Are you going to take him back to New York with you?" he sounded actually afraid that she would.

"No, of course not. While I love him dearly, I would never take him away from his brothers like that."

"Well, then where is he?"

"How would I know? I just got here." Now Cassie's fury was growing to match his, but she was trying valiantly to keep Ross from being hurt by the adults' anger.

When she cast a significant glance down toward the boy, Mr. Ainsworth seemed to gather himself.

"I apologize, Miss Morley. We are a little anxious at the moment. Of course you couldn't know where the boy is. If you will excuse us, we cannot entertain at the moment."

Cassie gasped at his attempt to be rid of her. "I am not going anywhere. I will help you search. I could never leave with this uncertainty about his safety."

Mr. Ainsworth glared at her but then his gaze once again took in the vision of Ross clinging to her and his stance softened. "Very well, just make sure you don't get in our way," he accepted gruffly.

Chapter Ten

C harles couldn't keep from staring at her. She was curled up with her feet tucked under her flowing skirts and Ross held firmly in her arms. They were both fast asleep. He knew it was worry exhausting them both added to the long day of searching. She hadn't complained about the grueling pace, only taking breaks when he forced her to. As he pointed out to her, it wouldn't do anyone any good to have her collapse on the trail; she'd only be an added burden to them then. When he had said that, she had flushed a deep red but had silently eaten the sandwich he had been pressing on her. And she offered no more argument whenever he had stopped her to offer her a drink or to suggest she take a moment to get off her horse when they stopped to water the horses.

It was obvious that guilt was eating at Cassie. Charles knew it wasn't her fault, but he didn't know how to convince her of that. The fact was the boy had disappeared after declaring he wanted to go stay with her. It wasn't her fault, but she was obviously having difficulty dealing with her involvement. If they didn't find the boy soon, they would all be consumed with guilt.

He was well aware that Walter's disappearance wasn't Cassie's fault — the fault firmly belonged on his shoulders. If he had been more aware of the boy's needs or not quite as dismissive of his attachment to Miss Cassie, Walter might not have run off.

His sigh must not have been as silent as he had hoped. While he watched, Cassie's eyes blinked open and she suddenly looked alert and concerned as she quickly realized where she was. Without disturbing the youngster in her arms, she sat up, still holding his gaze.

"Is there any news?"

Charles shook his head. "I'm sorry for disturbing you. You should try to get a little more sleep. You're obviously exhausted, and the boys are feeling comforted by your presence. I can't have you collapsing on me."

He realized his tone and words were less than gracious when she grimaced and turned her face away from him. He felt like kicking himself.

"I apologize, Miss Morley. I didn't mean to sound churlish. I mean to say that I'm glad you're here. Your presence is of benefit, but I don't want to see you getting sick from the strain. Get some more sleep, tomorrow might be just as difficult as today was."

He watched with a little bit of amusement as she blinked in surprise over his words. She was obviously still half asleep and wasn't about to start arguing with him over whether or not she was being of help. Charles knew that whether he liked her being there or not, until Walter was found there would be no way he could pry her away from his property. And she really was of help with Ross and Tony. Charles didn't know what he would have done with those two boys if not for her presence that day.

Still looking a little wary, Cassie snuggled back up with Ross and drifted back to sleep. Watching the two of them, Charles wanted to wake her back up and send her down the hall to a bed, but he hadn't the heart to disturb her again. He just hoped she wasn't too sore to ride in the morning.

∞ ∞

Cassie swam toward consciousness as the first rays of dawn filtered through the window. Being careful not to disturb the still deeply asleep little boy in her arms, she extricated herself from him with difficulty given how stiff she was. It took some effort, but she managed to regain her feet without waking Ross. She was amazed she had managed to get as much sleep as she had and gingerly stretched herself into alertness. She wished she had thought to pack a bag for herself when she had rode frantically into town the day before seeking any information on Walter. No one had seen him and she had left word with her two friends and at the hotel and smithy before racing back out to the Ainsworth property. It sure would be nice to have a fresh change of clothes, but that was a rather petty thought when the dear boy was still missing in the vast wilderness that stretched out as far as she could see from the wide window in the brightening light.

She was so lost in thought she nearly squealed when Mr. Ainsworth broke the stillness with his words.

"Did you manage to get much sleep?" His solicitous tone almost made him seem human. Yesterday as they had searched the buildings and he had bullied her into accepting his offers of food and water, she had doubted his humanity and marveled at his strength.

"More than I would have expected," she admitted with a grimace as she stretched a crick out of her neck.

"Were you terribly uncomfortable?" he asked before adding, "I should have sent you to a proper bed last night, but the two of you looked to be offering each other the comfort you needed so I didn't have the heart to disturb you."

Again Cassie was surprised by his words but didn't question them. "Don't worry about me. I'll be fine once I get a little blood flowing into some of my limbs. And maybe a little bit of that," she added with a grin as she watched him take a swig of what smelled like strong coffee.

He immediately handed her his cup before he noticed her hesitation. Cassie was surprised to see him blush.

"I'm so sorry! I will, of course, pour you a fresh cup," he exclaimed before bustling away.

Cassie burst into quiet giggles as she followed him from the room, not wanting to wake up Ross, who was still sleeping on the sofa she had shared with him.

When she arrived in the kitchen, Mr. Ainsworth was pouring her a fresh cup of coffee. From the smell she could tell that it was going to be very strong. She didn't usually drink the dark brew, but she knew she could use the help in clearing the cobwebs from her mind. She didn't bother commenting on his embarrassment, although she thought it would have been something to tease him about if they were friends. That thought made her sad but she tried to ignore it.

She bustled about the kitchen helping to make breakfast, conscious of Charles' gaze following her. She couldn't tell if it was censorious or not so she chose to ignore it. Before long they were ready to head out and search some more.

The day dragged on with no news. They had ridden out from the main area, searching wherever they could think to look. They also rode out to the neighbors to ask if he had been seen and to search their buildings.

As dusk was gathering on the second day of his disappearance, Cassie was beginning to despair. Once again Ross was in tears and she was losing her own fight against weeping. Sitting on the front stairs of Ainsworth's house, she had the youngster on her lap and was rubbing circles on his back trying to calm him. Tony was sitting beside them trying to be stoic, but Cassie could see his lower lip beginning to tremble.

Putting her arm around Tony, she gathered both boys as close to her heart as possible and tried to think what to say. As she herself was nearing despair, she couldn't make them any promises.

"We need to stay strong now, boys. We aren't giving up. Someone will surely have seen him."

"We never should have left New York, Miss Cassie," Tony declared. "It's too big and empty out here. In the city hundreds of people would have seen him by now."

Cassie sighed. "I know, Tony, but in the city many of those hundreds of people could have hurt him, too."

"You don't think there are bad men out here in Missouri?" he asked, scoffing.

She had no answer for him and felt her own tears finally give way. Ainsworth had been eavesdropping on their conversation as usual and chose that moment to sit down beside Tony and pull the three of them into his arms. His action stopped her tears, clogging her throat as she almost choked on her surprise.

"Come now, all of you. Do not despair. We'll find that rascal and bring him home safe and sound in a jiffy."

"He's not a rascal," Ross mumbled through his slowing tears.

"Sure he is," Ainsworth answered with a false note of joviality in his tone. "Leaving us all here to worry about him. Perhaps he's off having a good laugh at our expense right this minute."

Cassie was shocked. She tried to pull away from him, but he kept his grip firm. She turned to look at him, aware that her dismay over his words was probably written all over her face.

"You don't seriously believe that do you?" she demanded.

"No! I don't think he's hiding from us, but I do think we will find him. But we cannot give up or give in to despair. We need to rest up and keep searching again tomorrow."

His tone was warm but firm, and Cassie began to feel comforted by his grip. She laid her head on his shoulder over and around Tony. It felt as though they were a unit, sharing their fears and drawing strength from their mutual feelings. She tried to maintain a grip on her heart as it picked up its pace being this close to the handsome man. *He's just offering you comfort, you ninny*, she reminded herself. *Don't get carried away.*

Chapter Eleven

T he next morning everything fell down around them. Cassie awoke with a start. Tony was standing at the end of her bed with his anxious gaze fixed upon her. It was immediately obvious to her that he didn't want to wake her up, but he had something to tell her. She sat up and beckoned him close.

"What has happened?"

He was trying to be tough, but she could see how upset he was.

"It's all right, Tony. We'll figure it out. You don't have to carry this burden by yourself. Tell me what has happened."

"Someone is asking Mr. Charles for lots of money if he wants to get Walter back."

"They are?" Cassie was stunned. "Why would they ask Mr. Charles for money?"

Tony's lip trembled and she was instantly contrite. She quickly overrode her own demands in order to deal with the boy's concerns. "Come here, Tony," she commanded softly, holding her arms open. With a soft sob he practically jumped into her arms.

"What if he doesn't want to pay it?" he asked in a small voice.

"Why would you ask that? Of course he would want to pay it," was her immediate answer.

"But we just got here and it's turning out to be too much trouble."

"Oh, my dear boy, Mr. Charles knows this isn't Walter's fault, or yours or Ross's. You aren't being too much trouble. I am absolutely certain he will want to pay it." She placed gentle emphasis on the word want. She didn't mean to, but she couldn't imagine that the rancher would have any amount of extra money available to pay a ransom for the boy no matter how much he might want to pay it. She would have to contact her father. It would take considerable begging, but she would do anything for Walter. She just hoped she could be sufficiently convincing in a telegraph. And that he would be able to arrange the money for her quickly.

When the boy seemed calmer, Cassie got up and went in search of Mr. Ainsworth.

"Mr. Ainsworth?" she asked tentatively.

"Oh, surely you can call me Charles by now, can't you, Cassandra?"

Her hot blush scorched her cheeks. His impatience combined with the use of her given name confused her. It wasn't the time to argue so she pressed on, ignoring his words.

"Tony said there has been a ransom demand."

He cast his searching gaze over her before handing her the sheet of paper.

She couldn't open it just yet. She had some questions first. "All this time I've been thinking he wandered off and is lost or a wild animal got him. But now that there's a note from someone, it makes me wonder. Do you think this could be one of the townsfolk?"

Charles' gaze sharpened on her in question. "Why would you ask that?"

"The first day I came out here to visit the boys, the man at the smithy said some strange things about you. About the size of your property. It struck me at the time that he was probably jealous of you. Jealousy can cause people to do some terrible things."

"I agree that jealousy can cause people to be cruel and awful, but I really don't think the smithy had anything to do with Walter's disappearance."

"How can you be sure?" Cassie wanted to trust his judgement, but all the possibilities terrified her.

"For one thing, despite how he might feel about my land, I actually consider the smithy to be a friend. For another, I'm not completely sure the man is literate."

Cassie looked back down at the paper in her hand and finally forced herself to open it. Her eyes quickly scanned the missive.

"One thousand silver dollars?" she exclaimed and then had to sit down. That was as far as her eyes had gotten. She gazed at him without comprehension. "How can this be happening?"

"Don't worry, Cassie, we'll get Walter back. Don't you see, this is good news?"

"How can you say this is good news?" Her eyes had returned to the paper she held. "They are demanding the money by tomorrow evening. I can't abide the thought of Walter being with these blackguards another moment, but I don't know how I will be able to get the money by tomorrow evening."

She could feel tears welling up in her eyes but couldn't turn away when she saw the arrested expression on his face. "What do you mean YOU can't get the money?" he asked in an odd voice. "You might have noticed that it was not you from whom they have demanded the ransom."

Cassie felt hot color staining her cheeks once more. "Well, no, perhaps it was not addressed to me, but surely I must have access to more money through my father..." She trailed off, quailing under his incredulous stare. She returned her eyes to the paper in her hands.

"Actually, it would appear that it isn't addressed to either of us. Who is Gibby? And why would they be speaking to him about Walter?" She could hear her voice becoming shrill but was powerless to stop it.

Charles knelt before her and grasped her hands. "Shhh, Cassie, it's going to be all right, don't worry."

"But how?" She wanted to trust him and found his warm grasp comforting but was overwhelmed by her fear for Walter. "Do they even say where he is or why they are doing this?" She still held the paper, but it was crumpled with Charles holding her hand. "And where are we going to get the money? And where are we supposed to leave it?"

Again Charles tried to quiet her fears. "Shhh, you have to calm down, Cassie. Take a deep breath."

Cassie did as he said. She joined in his laughter when he started to laugh and reminded her, "All right, now let it out or you'll faint on me."

She almost squirmed under his penetrating gaze while she continued taking deep, fortifying breaths. He must have decided she was calm enough because he got up from the crouch he was in before her and sat beside her while still holding on to one of her hands.

"Thank you, Mr. Ainsworth." Upon noting his censorious expression she colored slightly and corrected herself. "That is, Charles, I appreciate your patience with me. I'm sure you are just as anxious as the rest of us about Walter and have had just as little sleep. I shouldn't have lost my composure like that."

"I shan't hold it against you. It was perfectly understandable."

"But what ARE we going to do, Charles? I'm relieved to read that Walter hasn't been carried off by some wild animal as I had feared, but if someone is holding him for ransom, we need to get him back."

"I agree with you wholeheartedly, Cassandra, but I don't think paying the ransom is the answer."

Cassie could only stare blankly at him. "Whatever do you mean? Of course we have to pay it!"

Charles patted her hand, reminding her not to lose her presence of mind. Cassie kept her voice low, not wanting the boys to hear their discussion.

"Walter has been missing for almost three days. We cannot be sure this note is actually from a kidnapper. It could be someone taking advantage of our tragedy. We cannot just bring a large sum of money and hand it over without proof that Walter is alive."

Cassie could see the wisdom of his words. "But how are we going to arrange that?" While waiting for his answer, she disengaged her hand from his grasp and spread open the ransom note, scanning it for more information. "It's not signed. I wonder if that's a message in itself. Have you ever encountered a situation like this?" She searched his gaze. "I have to ask, Charles, why are you so calm? Is it just that you're trying to be manly and strong for me and the boys or are you somehow experienced in these types of matters?"

This prompted another laugh from Charles. "No, I cannot say that I have ever had anyone demand ransom money from me before."

Cassie felt like she was in a fog and kept staring at the paper in her hands. "Why would they write Dear Gibby?" she mused. "That is decidedly strange. Do you know anyone named Gibby?" She finally looked up at Charles and was surprised to see the discomfort on his face that he was trying to hide from her. "What is it, Charles? What aren't you telling me? Who is Gibby?"

When he didn't immediately answer her, she turned the paper over, hoping there would be more information on the other side. There was. In a messy scrawl, where it would have been visible when the page was folded in three, was a name – Gibson Charles

Ainsworth Emerson – and she felt certain pieces of the puzzle shift into place and all the blood drain from her head.

"You're Gibson Emerson?" she asked, accusation evident in her tone. She wanted to laugh hysterically but tried not to get sidetracked from the point at hand. It was obvious by his continued silence that he didn't want to talk about his name issues. "Since this is apparently not the name you go by, whoever sent this letter knows more about you than you would like. Who in these parts might know this? And are you aware of anyone who might call you Gibby? Which is a horrible appellation, if you ask me."

Again Charles laughed. It had a hollow tone to it, but at least he was no longer keeping silent. "You aren't nearly as empty headed as you would like New York society to think, are you, Cassandra Morley?" he asked in a quiet, admiring voice.

Cassie could only stare at him disdainfully. Charles sighed. "I would have to agree with you. I've always hated it if anyone calls me Gibby. The only person who insists upon it is my cousin, Cedric."

"I know he is the black sheep of your family, but do you think he would stoop so low as to kidnap a child?" she asked. She could hear the chill in her tone but couldn't be bothered to disguise it.

"I wouldn't have thought so, but I wouldn't put it past him, either. On the other hand, since he has been highly resentful of my successes in life, he could just be taking advantage of this adversity and may not actually have Walter but is just hoping to relieve me of some of my funds, since he is always with his pockets to let."

Cassie was furious but was trying valiantly to keep it in check. It wasn't Charles or Gibson or whatever his name is, it wasn't his fault his cousin was a wretch. "Do you have any idea how we might get in touch with dear cousin Cedric?" she asked in a restrained voice. "Or if we could ascertain if he does, in fact, have Walter?"

"Do you remember the men who were watching us when we went for a ride the day before Walter went missing? I know you noticed them even though you didn't say anything."

Cassie frowned, unsure why he was answering her question with more questions. "Yes, I remember."

"I'm pretty sure those men are associates of my cousin."

Cassie felt the bottom drop out of her stomach. She had been hoping that somehow this situation could be cleared up easily. Those men had made her uncomfortable that day. She hated to think how terrified Walter must be if he were in their clutches. She went back to the slow, deep, measured breaths she had been taking in an effort to control her reaction.

When she felt that she had herself in hand she asked, "Why did you not say something sooner? Did you suspect them from the beginning?"

"One never wants to suspect their own family of stabbing them in the back, metaphorically speaking. I was suspicious of those rough looking men. It was too coincidental that he disappeared the day after they were watching us, but I wouldn't have imagined Cedric's involvement until I received that letter. I still cannot say for sure if he actually has Walter or if he's just wallowing in my pain. I would expect kidnappers to demand ransom immediately, not wait a few days."

"He was always into torture, if I recall correctly. You should have seen what he did to my doll on the one occasion that I had the misfortune of meeting him when I was a child." Cassie paused and watched Charles assimilate the fact that she knew who Cedric was. "So tell me, Gibby," she said with sarcastic emphasis, "what are you going to do now?"

She was surprised and slightly mollified to see color creep into his cheeks but would not allow herself to soften toward him. She had been so worried Walter's disappearance was her fault, but it had been his all along. He should have known his terrible cousin had a hand in this. But then she was horrified by the remembrance as he had pointed out that Cedric might not have

Walter at all. She tried not to panic and waited to see what he had to say.

"I've already dispatched messengers to wherever I can think of to find Cedric. And I will send telegraphs to my aunt and parents to see if they have any information on his whereabouts if my messengers come up empty handed." He paused and searched her face. "I swear to you, we will get to the bottom of this *and* bring Walter home safely before much more time has passed."

"But what if, as you say, Cedric doesn't actually have him and this is just an unnecessary diversion?" Cassie grimaced over the quaver she heard in her voice, but it could not be helped. She held Charles' gaze and willed her lips not to quiver.

"I know I said that, and I cannot say why he would wait to send the ransom note, but we have looked everywhere. Surely someone has taken the boy and no one else has claimed responsibility, so it is only reasonable to think Cedric must have him."

Cassie nodded but felt sick to her stomach. "So now there's nothing to do but wait, it would seem." She felt as though she had aged at least a decade in the last three days. "I had best go and see if I can distract Ross and Tony while we try to keep our hopes up. Thank you for your patience with all my questions."

෨〇ඏ

Charles watched as the young woman left the room, admiring as she tried valiantly to hide her mixed emotions. It was obvious she was furious with him for hiding his identity from her. And of course, she was sick over his involvement in Walter's disappearance. But he was impressed that she had the sense to realize that now was not the time to raise a fuss about it. All their energies needed to be focused on rescuing the boy. Recriminations could wait until he was safe. He hoped she would be able to keep the brothers busy while he saw to dealing with Cedric. It turned Charles' stomach to think that his own cousin would be so nefarious, but he couldn't focus on that at the moment or he could lose his mental dexterity. He would have to keep his emotions at arm's length to see them all through the next days and bring Walter home. He thought again of Cassie and realized that it would take more effort than he would have thought to hold back his feelings. Who would have thought that he would care about a socialite's opinion?

Chapter Twelve

C harles stood in the hallway listening as Cassie read to the boys. It was a story of rollicking adventure, sure to keep the boys' minds occupied while the adults dealt with their missing brother. And her manner of reading would keep them captivated, he thought as he realized that he too was becoming preoccupied.

Shaking his head, he walked quietly away and left the house. He hated to leave them but he was hoping to keep the rest of the proceedings away from those three. He didn't want them marred by the ugliness that might follow. He knew Cassie would probably want to be involved, but he thought it was for the best if he could keep her from it. His heart constricted slightly at how natural it was to leave his boys in her care. *Perhaps Walter had been right, and we need to keep Cassie here with us*, he thought wistfully. He pushed the thought from his mind — he needed to keep his focus on the task at hand.

It was perfect timing. As soon as he stepped onto the porch he spotted one of the men he had sent out for information returning and looking purposeful. He was glad to intercept him before he could knock on the door.

"You look like you have some news, Brad."

"I do, sir. I found where Cedric and several others are holed up in a rundown shack on the outskirts of the next town over. I asked around as discretely as possible. Seems they were asking for milk at the mercantile. I doubt that sort has taken to drinking milk, so I'm thinking they do have the boy after all."

Charles almost sagged with relief but couldn't give in to the wave of emotion. Now the really tricky part was to begin. How could they rescue the boy without anyone getting hurt?

ℴℴ

Sitting back firmly into his saddle, Charles looked around at the men. Those he could see were all in position. The ones he couldn't see, behind the small, rough building, he trusted implicitly so he knew they were where he asked them to be. All would go as well as could be hoped when dealing with a rough customer like Cedric and his associates. Charles couldn't figure out for the life of him why the bounder had chosen to follow him to Missouri. They had never gotten along. With the vastness of this land it was ridiculous for his cousin to seek him out. Of course, it could just be, as he had told Cassie, that his cousin just wanted to cause him trouble.

Glancing to his right, Charles was glad to have the sheriff by his side. His family back East wouldn't be happy about it, but he wasn't going to give Cedric a pass when he had attacked Charles right in his home – there was no forgiveness for taking one of his sons.

The plan was simple. They were counting on the element of surprise. And outnumbering their opponents. He just prayed Walter would have the sense to take cover and not get hurt in the process.

After a nod from the sheriff, Charles dropped his raised hand and all the men advanced at once upon the shack. Within minutes it was over. Seeing as it was late in the afternoon, Cedric's men had already drunk themselves into a stupor. They couldn't respond quickly enough when Charles and his men had broken in from all directions. The shack had completed its collapse when some of Charles' ranch hands had kicked a space for themselves to enter from the back. Thankfully, Walter had been huddled in a corner and didn't sustain any injuries. The sheriff's deputy had a grin on his face as he quickly tied up the three men who had been following Cedric. Of course, Cedric was nowhere to be found. Charles gritted his teeth at the thought that the brute might get away free. As long as he kept himself far from Charles' family, he supposed he didn't much care what became of his cousin. And for the sake of family relations it might be for the best if he wasn't responsible for his cousin's arrest. Charles shook his head. He wasn't responsible in any case. He had certainly not asked the ruffian to make off with his son.

Speaking of the boy, Charles quickly gathered the youngster into his arms and strode from the debris of the shack while his men helped the sheriff with the criminals. Settling himself against a tree, he took a deep breath before looking intently at the boy. He would've fallen over from the shock if he wasn't already sitting.

Having expected to see fear or panic on the boy's face, Charles wasn't prepared to see Walter's bright shining eyes and huge grin. He burst into laughter.

"Shouldn't you be panicking or something?"

"That was swell, Mr. Charles!!"

"That's not how I would describe it, but I'm glad to see that you weren't afraid." Charles examined the child for any signs of injury or harm. "Did they hurt you in any way?" Now that the boy was safe, he was feeling the reaction to all the fears he had kept hidden. He wanted to squeeze the boy to his heart and never let him go, but the youngster's lack of distress was mixing up his feelings.

The boy's grin began to fade, and he couldn't meet Charles' gaze. "I was scared some of the time, Mr. Charles. I didn't think you would come for me, especially when I heard them talking about asking someone for money for me. It didn't make much sense, but I thought maybe Miss Cassie would come if she knew I was taken."

"She has been trying to find you, along with me and your brothers. She is going to be furious when she finds out that we left her behind when we came for you."

This helped to restore Walter's grin. "She'll probably have some words for you, Mr. Charles."

Chapter Thirteen

Walter had been correct in his assessment. Cassie was furious when she realized Charles had left without her. When she couldn't find him anywhere in the house, she had gone outside to look for him. Hank, the farm hand who had been left behind to watch over the ranch while everyone else rode out to rescue Walter, had been a little bitter when he informed her of his whereabouts.

"Left me here to see to you all," Hank had said in such an aggrieved tone of voice that Cassie would have laughed if she didn't feel similarly.

"I'm terribly sorry that you were left behind, Hank. I cannot believe that Mr. Ainsworth would stoop so low as to trick me into staying behind."

"He wasn't being low toward you, miss. He's that concerned about keeping you safe. Seems to me, you ought to be grateful."

Cassie made every effort not to be offended by the man's words. He was just trying to be honest and defend his employer. He certainly wasn't trying to hurt her feelings. And he was even hurt himself for having been left behind. She offered him a tight smile.

"I'm sorry you are stuck with us. We will make every effort not to cause you any difficulty."

A few hours later, when they heard the sound of many hoofbeats entering the yard, Cassie felt as though her nerves had frayed. She wanted to yell like a fishwife at Charles for leaving them behind with no explanation. Needing to keep Ross and Tony entertained, while not knowing if Walter and Charles were safe, had nearly done her in.

Cassie could tell he felt guilty by the way he wouldn't make eye contact with her when she shot a glare his way. But she couldn't hold onto her anger for long in the face of her joy at being reunited with Walter. The boy's safety meant everything to her. *How am I ever going to leave them behind?* Despite how angry she was toward Charles, she knew he was included in the "them" she would mourn the loss of when she returned to New York.

Cassie could barely bring herself to let go of Walter but she realized in order to help him overcome his ordeal she would have to try to hide the depth of her own feelings. She forced herself to smile brightly as she released him from her tight hug. He looked at her seriously.

"It's all right, Miss Cassie, you can squeeze me a little more, I don't mind."

This sent her off in a peal of giggles. Everyone joined her, and the tension that had accumulated quickly dissipated as they all laughed their relief.

"Are you hungry? We could make you whatever you would like to eat," she offered, determined not to hover.

Her heart rolled over when he smiled sweetly at her. "I would be happy to eat some pancakes, please."

She couldn't resist; she bent down and placed a brief kiss gently on his brow. "There will be plenty of pancakes served momentarily. I think we could all use some sweetness right about now."

Cassie had been hoping for a moment or two alone to collect her thoughts and pull herself together emotionally, but the whole gang followed her to the kitchen. Walter didn't want to be away from Cassie while the other two boys weren't letting Walter out of their sight, and it seemed as though Charles didn't want to be left by himself. The four males made themselves comfortable while Cassie bustled around the kitchen.

There was a moment of uncomfortable silence behind her but then Cassie heard Tony asking Walter about his experience.

"Were you scared?"

"Of course not," the youngster declared. Cassie rolled her eyes and had to resist turning to see the other boys' reactions.

"Well, I was scared," Tony admitted while Ross added, "I even cried."

"Really?" Walter seemed shocked that his brothers would admit as much. There was a heartbeat of silence before he continued. "At first I didn't even realize what was happening. I thought it was a joke or something. The men were talking about Mr. Charles, so I thought they were ranch hands that I just hadn't met yet. But they weren't very nice. By the time I realized what was happening, I was too mad to be scared or even to cry, even though I wanted to, especially at night."

"Why were you mad?" Tony wanted to know. "How could you be too mad to be scared?"

"I figured I would get in trouble for running away and it would be their fault."

Cassie snorted trying not to laugh and tried to cover it up by coughing. She almost jumped out of her skin when a soft voice at her shoulder admonished, "You need to be quieter if you want to take up eavesdropping as a pastime."

She whirled to confront Charles, furious that he would startle her when they had all barely begun to recover from their earlier frights. He must have realized his blunder because he was immediately contrite.

"I apologize profusely, Cassie, I didn't realize you were unaware that I was beside you. I didn't mean to surprise you." He gave her a significant glance. "Now, please point that knife somewhere else."

She glanced down and realized she still held a knife clenched in her hand. She laughed softly. "I had just started peeling some apples." She followed through and continued with her task before glancing at him with apprehension. "I hope you don't mind that I have made myself at home in your kitchen without even asking your leave. It was the first thing I thought of, the need to feed the boys, and didn't even think to ask if you would mind."

"Don't even give it a thought. I don't mind at all. I don't think any of us have eaten properly in at least three days. Besides you look far better in here than I do. And from what I've seen in the last day or two, you are far more skilled than my cook."

"For a socialite, you mean?" she couldn't help asking.

He laughed. "You are definitely far more skilled than any socialite I've ever met. And I suppose I owe you an apology for having judged you so harshly when I first met you after so many years. I realize you had no idea who I was, but I recognized you almost immediately. Even before I heard your name, I was pretty sure you were Mitch Morley's daughter. The set of your jaw when you stepped off the train was exactly how he would look when he was considering a new business arrangement."

Cassie laughed. "Oh dear. Did I look terribly arrogant?"

Charles joined her laughter. "Not arrogant, just determined. And I now realize you were trying to hide all your misgivings behind a layer of bravado. I wonder if that's your father's strategy," he trailed off.

"I doubt it. Father always knows what he's doing. Or thinks he's right even if he doesn't know." She grinned. "But you are correct. I had no idea who you were. I was only four or five when I saw you last, and I had no thought that there could possibly be a family acquaintance out here in Missouri. No one has mentioned it. I had quite forgotten about your existence in fact," she added with another grin. "Besides the fact that you are going by a different name out here. I haven't yet had the chance to ask you about that." She could feel his eyes watching her closely as she whisked together the apples, setting them to simmer with sugar to make a warm sauce for the pancakes. Cassie willed her hands not to shake while she measured the flour and other ingredients. Her nerves were already shot from worrying about Walter. She could barely tolerate Charles' scrutiny. She was relieved that her question caused him to shift his eyes away as he pondered how best to answer her.

"I was fairly disillusioned when I left New York. My parents' wealth had so many strings attached to it. I didn't want to be a puppet on the end of those strings, so I set out to make my own way in the world. I was determined that anything I accomplished was going to be on my own merit, so I needed a new name. I didn't want to be completely disloyal, though, so I chose two of the names my parents had given me, just not the ones anyone would recognize or associate with them."

"Well, your ploy worked. I even know your family, and I didn't realize you were you." She paused while she carefully broke a couple eggs into her bowl, ignoring his amused grin over her need to concentrate. "Don't make fun, Charles. I am sure you realize I haven't actually spent too very much time in a kitchen."

"I would never have guessed. You seem right at home."

"Never mind that, I need to ask you something. Did you end up having to telegraph your family to find out anything about Cedric? I forgot to ask you earlier."

"No, I didn't, but why do you ask?"

Cassie sighed. "I would ever so much rather my parents never discover that I met you out here. You will remain Charles Ainsworth in my recounting of any of my adventures in Missouri."

"That still doesn't answer my question." When Cassie searched his face, he appeared genuinely puzzled.

"Are you being deliberately obtuse or have you been gone from New York too long?"

"That is doing nothing to clear up my confusion, Cassie, but it is certainly making me all the more intrigued to know what you mean."

Cassie sighed again. "If it is ever found out that I encountered an Emerson bachelor and did not manage to ensnare you, I will be deemed utterly too stupid to live." There was a pause where she contemplated this melancholy thought but then she brightened. "On the other hand, perhaps they will realize I am a completely lost cause and will give up on trying to force me into the mold they have designated for my life."

Charles gazed at her in silence while she fidgeted with the pancake batter. He finally broke his silence. "Why bother going back to New York?"

"I can't stay here. I don't have skills like Katie and Melanie. They will be able to provide for themselves just fine. There's not much of a place for a New York socialite outside of New York."

"You've been pretty great here for the last three days, keeping our spirits up and insisting we sleep or eat, even when you yourself didn't want to. I would have lost my mind trying to keep Ross and Tony occupied and comforted while also searching for Walter and trouncing my cousin. I have come to realize that even boys need both a father and a mother."

Cassie blinked rapidly, trying to clear from her mind the idea that was beginning to form. She feigned amusement. "If I didn't know any better, I would suspect you were thinking that I might fill that role."

"You can't tell me you don't want it or that you wouldn't be any good at it, even if you are a little too young to actually be their mother."

She felt hot color flood her face from her neck to the roots of her hair. "I would love to be the boys' mother, but the title of mother most often accompanies that of wife, and I know nothing about that." She couldn't look at him as she busied herself with the stove. "Of course, you probably didn't think through what you are saying, so let us just pretend this conversation never happened."

He watched her fidget with her sauce under his lowered lids. "I actually did give this a great deal of thought over the last couple of days. I think you would make an exceptionally good wife." He paused briefly before adding, "And mother to my three sons."

They hadn't noticed that the boys were listening. "Yes, yes, yes, yes, yes!" exclaimed the three youngsters as they jumped up and down and began running around the kitchen.

Walter clasped his hands together and earnestly said, "This was worth getting kidnapped for."

Cassie could feel that the hot color was once again covering her face, but she laughed over Walter's words. "Never mind boys, this is not a conversation for you to participate in. Mr. Charles and I will finish discussing it after we have all enjoyed our pancakes."

It was perhaps her inexperience showing to suggest because it proved impossible to keep the topic from being discussed by the excited boys but thankfully they were too busy stuffing the delicious pancakes into their mouths to say too much. Their relief and joy lent them huge appetites, and Cassie was kept busy filling their plates. She only managed to force one small pancake down her own dry throat and it tasted like sawdust to her, but the males in the room seemed to be enjoying them so she didn't worry too much about her cooking, despite her discomfort with Charles' hot gaze following her constantly. She half expected that she would lose her mind and set the house on fire since she could barely pay attention to what she was doing.

Cassie was filled with half relief and half despair when the three boys were finally full and they asked to be excused. Charles granted permission and they hurried from the room. But not before Walter stopped beside her and whispered loudly, "Please say, yes, Miss Cassie," and then quickly followed his brothers.

Cassie could feel tears gathering in the corners of her eyes and tried to blink them away as she gathered up the plates and fidgeted around the kitchen. Her fidgets came to an abrupt end when Charles' warm hand closed over hers.

"Stop squirming around the topic. The boys have gone and left us to our private conversation. You are right to be irritated with me. I shouldn't have forced your hand by asking you with the boys in the room, but I thought they were fully occupied."

"But you didn't ask me anything," she protested, blushing.

He stared at her in amazement. After a brief, stunned silence, he gathered both of her hands into one of his large ones and then with his free hand he held her chin and forced her to meet his gaze.

"Cassandra Morley, would you please do me the great honor of being my wife?"

She could feel her chin trembling despite his warm grip on it. "But why would you want to marry me? You keep saying how little regard you have for New York socialites. Surely you would be better off with someone like Katie or Mel. They have skills far more suited to life in Missouri."

"Cass, don't be obtuse now. I've barely met Katie or Mel. But I have watched you carefully through what I expect was the most gruelling experience of your life. You remained kind, unselfish, and caring. I realize now that while you are from a wealthy New York family, you are not a socialite no matter what your mother might say. And that makes you uniquely suited to be my wife."

Cassie blinked at him. Her puzzlement must have been clearly written on her face. He sighed before elaborating. "Just as I can see you are not cut from the same cloth as the rest of your family, I most certainly am not like the rest of the Emmersons. Don't get me wrong, I have no interest in living as a Spartan. I'm happy to work hard and provide well for my family. I just refuse to be sucked into the showy lifestyle that my, and your, family seem to love. I have finally realized that you feel the same way."

When Cassie made to protest, he hushed her. "I know, you didn't always feel that way. I've heard you protest your questionable motivation for starting your work at the orphanage. But it is how you feel now, isn't it? You yourself said you don't want to be pushed into the mold your parents want you in."

She wasn't sure what to say to him in response. She merely nodded, keeping her wide eyes focused on him watchfully. He nodded firmly and continued. "You will fully understand my background and my complicated relationship with my family, but I know you will be a lovely partner for my life here, and you would be equal to the task if we ever decided, as a family, to return to the city. You are, in fact, perfect for me."

Cassie wasn't sure what to say. The past several days had been a whirlwind for her emotions. She wasn't sure if she should trust what he was saying. She wanted to believe him, but needed to be certain.

"Charles," she began before pausing to gather her thoughts.

"I will beg if I have to, but please, Cassie, be my wife."

She offered a watery chuckle as she fought emotional tears. "I might like to see that."

Charles grinned at her. "Are you trying to torture me as revenge for my cold reception to you when you first arrived in Bucklin?"

"Not at all, but you cannot argue with the fact that it seems to be a rather sudden change of heart. Is this just an emotional reaction to the stresses we've all faced with Walter's disappearance?"

Cassie was surprised by the emotions that quickly chased themselves across the handsome man's features before he showed her an impassive face. It slipped a little around the edges, but she was fairly certain she had hurt his feelings.

"I apologize if I have made you uncomfortable with my words. I can assure you, I am quite sure of my feelings. They are sound and stable, not brought on by our recent stresses."

Cassie allowed the silence that followed his words to lengthen as she studied his face carefully. He wasn't giving much away but she felt he was being sincere. She sighed softly. "The only thing is, Charles, you haven't actually told me what your feelings are. You mentioned that our backgrounds are compatible and you no longer consider me to be superficial. I am not completely convinced that is sufficient for building a life together so far from what is familiar to me."

The silence stretched out after her words while Charles frowned and thought over what she had said. Suddenly his face split into a grin and he eased down onto one knee. "Very well then, begging it is," he said with a chuckle. Cassie began to giggle but quickly sobered as he tightened his grip on her hands and his grin drifted into seriousness.

"Cassandra Morley, you are as lovely on the inside as you are on the outside. I may not have always shown it, but I found you delightful every time you came to visit the boys. I loved watching you struggle to be polite whenever I was being surly. Your patience with the boys as you helped teach them to ride made me want to pull you into my arms, even as I tried to keep you at arm's length. I didn't want to have any feelings for you because I was convinced your place was back in New York."

Cassie tried to prevent it, but tears were welling in her eyes as he expressed his thoughts to her. One solitary tear broke its confines and slid down her cheek. She didn't speak. He surged back to his feet, reaching out gently to wipe the tear away. "As hard as I fought my feelings, they continued to grow. You might not have much experience at country living or even running a household, but I have watched you, especially while Walter was missing. You make up for whatever you might lack in knowledge or experience with your intelligence, willingness, and enthusiasm. I am completely convinced that you could make a success of whatever you might put your mind to. I hope you might put your mind to making a life here with me, and with those three boys you love so much. Even more, I am most certain that, while you will be a wonderful mother to the boys we've already got and any more children that we might be blessed with, I look forward to spending an adventurous life with you long after the children have left home. I love you Cassie, and I want to spend the rest of my days with you by my side. If you need more time to figure out if you could possibly feel the same way, I will try to understand, but I reserve the right to work very hard at convincing you. Please say you'll have me."

With a delighted whoop of joy, Cassie pulled her hands from his grasp and threw them around his neck. "That is the loveliest thing anyone has ever said to me. I've been fighting my feelings for you ever since I met you. I didn't think you could possibly love me. But I can see what you're saying. We *are* uniquely suited. I can see that you love the boys and will be a wonderful father. More importantly, though, you understand where I have come from and will be able to help me adjust to this new life. I love you, too, Mr. Gibson Charles Ainsworth Emmerson," she declared with a giggle while he growled at her.

"We needn't be so formal. Charles will do." He squeezed her tight.

In his tight hold, she didn't have much air, but she couldn't find it in herself to care. She didn't want to be anywhere else. With laughter filled with pure joy, she finally gave him the answer he was waiting for. "Yes, please, Charles, I would very much love to be your wife."

Charles had already been squeezing the breath out of her, but after one quick, tighter squeeze, he loosened his grasp and one of his hands came up to cradle the back of her head. Cassie was already feeling lightheaded from being in his arms, but now, as their breath mingled and his eyes stared hotly into hers, she felt as though her legs would have given out if not for the fact that his other arm was still wrapped around her. She was already up on her tiptoes, now it felt as though her feet weren't even touching the floor. He started at the corner of her eye, placing a soft kiss just where it was crinkled up from her wide smile. Then he trailed down to her cheekbone with a feather-light kiss there. She held her breath as he moved again.

His lips were a hairsbreadth away from hers when he whispered once more, "I love you, Cassie." And then there were no more words as he sealed their bargain with the press of his lips. He tasted of coffee and sweet applesauce and something else that could only be uniquely him. A multitude of thoughts chased each other around her head in the split second before she could no longer think as they enjoyed the sweet moment.

They broke away to catch their breath, but he continued to hold her securely in his embrace. Cassie threw her head back and laughed. "My parents will have to forgive me after all. I managed to catch myself an Emmerson."

Charles joined her in shared laughter before his lips descended onto hers once more.

The End

Read the next book in the *Orphan Train* series,

Katie

Can she risk love without sacrificing her independence?

Stay in touch with Wendy May Andrews
and forthcoming publishing news.

Sign up for her biweekly newsletter on
wendymayandrews.com

Married by Proxy

Another series set in the mid-west you will love:

They didn't meet until after the wedding day.

Carter McLain has finally accomplished the success he was striving for when he moved to the frontier a decade ago. All that's missing is a wife to share it with. Having no desire to leave his land, he requests a friend back home to arrange a proxy marriage for him. When his bride seems too good to be true, Carter wonders if he did the right thing.

The highly publicized deaths of Ella St. Clair's parents cause her to lose everything. Left destitute, alone, and friendless, she grudgingly accepts the offer of marriage by proxy to a man she has never met. The long trip West leaves her plenty of time for second thoughts.

What does the future hold for these legally bound strangers? Can they get past their secrets to find happiness?

This is a sweet, wholesome historical romance featuring a smart, strong heroine and the brooding hero who steals her heart. Download today and get ready to fall in love.

To buy please visit wendymayandrews.com

About the Author

I've been writing pretty much since I learned to read when I was five years old. Of course, those early efforts were basically only something a mother could love. I put writing aside after I left school and stuck with reading. I am an avid reader. I love words. I will read anything, even the cereal box, signs, posters, etc. But my true love is novels.

Eight or nine years ago my husband dared me to write a book instead of always reading them. I didn't think I'd be able to do it, but to my surprise I love writing. Those early efforts eventually became my first published book – Tempting the Earl (published by Avalon books in 2010). There were some ups and downs in my publishing efforts. My first publisher was sold and I became an "orphan" author, back to the drawing board of trying to find a publishing house. It has been a thrilling adventure as I learned to navigate the world of publishing.

I believe firmly that everyone deserves a happily ever after. I want my readers to be able to escape from the everyday for a little while and feel upbeat and refreshed when they get to the end of my books.

Stay in touch:

Website: www.wendymayandrews.com

Facebook: www.facebook.com/WendyMayAndrews

Instagram: www.instagram.com/WendyMayAndrews

Twitter: www.twitter.com/WendyMayAndrews